THERE WAS A FORTUNE IN GOLD hidden somewhere in those hills and valleys. But the terrible Aahasi with his fanatic braves guarded the canyon well. There were many scalps to prove it, and there would be many more.

The tough cowhands and the hired guns watched with amusement as Rogett rode off to the forbidden land. They'd seen others like him leave, some confident, some cocky—and none of them were ever heard from again.

THE SECRET
OF
APACHE CANYON

RICHARD TELFAIR

A FAWCETT GOLD MEDAL BOOK • NEW YORK

THE SECRET OF APACHE CANYON

© 1959 CBS Publications,
The Consumer Publishing Division of CBS Inc.

ISBN: 0-449-13985-9

Printed in the United States of America

14   13   12   11   10   9   8   7   6   5

Chapter One

THEY HAD A SAYING in Jicarilla, a small town that has long since disappeared from the New Mexico hills west of the Rio Grande but east of the continental divide: *When the heat hits a hundred and twenty-five, Jezebel is throwing a fit in hell;* the saying could be heard often where the miners congregated in the saloons with the cattlemen and riders for the big outfits.

And if you were a stranger in the mining center and cross-roads for the southern Arizona-to-Santa Fe stage, someone was bound to add a second saying, another part of the same legend that had been traded back and forth for twenty-five years as the question of Jezebel. The second saying was more enigmatic than the first: *The treasure of Aahasi lingers yet for the one that will dig in the shadows before the sun rises.*

"That's interesting," Rogett said to his host as they sat on the east veranda sipping coffee and watching the long shadows creep across the grass. "Where did it originate?"

His host, a slight man who sported a well-trimmed beard, removed his cigar and poked it accusingly at the shadow that was closing in fast on the nest of foothills before the broader range of mountains. The mountains themselves were outlined against the dark reflected reddish hue cast by the sinking sun against the high bank of clouds. Rogett was quiet. He wondered if his host, who he had discovered to be a hard-driving business man, was going to speak. He now wished, fretfully, that he had not allowed himself to be persuaded to remain overnight. He could have taken the stage to Santa Fe and been well on his way back to the East before dawn.

He sipped his coffee and made a face. They brewed it like mud. And they drank it constantly.

He threw a cautious glance at his host, wondering if he should ask about the saying again and noticed the sudden movement of the man, a forward thrusting of his jaw, eyes gleaming, his hands tight on the arm of the chair, as he watched the mountains dissolve into the coming night.

They were sure queer, this bunch, Rogett thought. Well, one couldn't really blame them. Living in the wilderness, with rattlesnakes in the front yard (they had killed one only an hour before not ten feet from the steps of the veranda), the ugly gila monsters that looked like something out of a nightmare, and Indians that were still holding out against the move of the whites and the government troops. Rogett shivered. He wished more than ever that he had gone on to Santa Fe.

He cleared his throat, not intending it as a reminder to his host, but the little man snapped back and rocked several times and puffed rapidly on his cigar. "Sorry," the host said.

They were silent again for a long time and Rogett shifted uncomfortably in the rocker.

"This is a funny country, Mistuh Rogett."

Rogett started to agree and then thought it better to remain quiet. Funny was not the word for it, the beleaguered Bostonian thought. Well, it had been worth the effort. He had always wanted to see the "wild West" and he had certainly seen it. Enough for a lifetime. He patted the freshly executed contract for the mining concession in his pocket and settled back to suffered whatever would come as a hidden demand in the business of doing business.

The host got up and Rogett was again struck with the ramrod-straight, cold-eyed demeanor of the man. Behind him were the distant sounds of Spanish voices and the rattle of kitchenware signaling dinner. The repeated invita-

6

tion to join in "a chunk of bloody beef and sour dough biscuits", which was the host's way of insisting that Rogett remain for another night, worked strange things in his stomach and he wondered if he would be able to eat anything at all.

A good night's sleep, he thought, and then off! Thank God!

His host struck a kitchen match to light a fresh cigar, and Rogett could see even more sharply the chiseled features of the man. A sharp, clean line to the nose, hard, bright eyes, clear skin that was burned brown from years of exposure, and a quickness in the movements that bespoke a sound muscle tone. He was no more than five feet six inches tall, not including the three-inch Texas heels of his boots, and his hands were large, much too large for a man his size, and thick through the palm. There was a jagged, ugly red scar on the back of his right hand that Rogett had been aching to inquire about, and another thick scar on his neck that ran from his right eye to a mysterious depth beyond the edge of his shirt collar.

The Colt the man wore looked old, and the leather holster even older. Rogett looked secretly at the butt to see if there were any notches, but the handle was smooth and worn. The Bostonian wondered if his host could dangle the thing around his finger the way he had heard some of them in the West could do. And was he quick on the draw?

But he would never ask these questions.

Twenty-two thousand acres of the finest grazing land in New Mexico. Plenty of water, protected by the mountains from the heavy winter and every foot of it fenced in with five-strand wire. A personal holding that Rogett had estimated to be worth at least five million dollars, when one included the cattle, horses, and the potential in the mine his company was going to open. The cash and blue chip bonds his host was reputed to hold could add another two million. And there was talk—and Rogett was not sure now that it was talk of a gossipy nature—about the holdings of his host in British Allied Trust.

Rogett was not a poor man himself. He controlled, or

7

owned outright, property and securities that would bring two million if he had to convert to cash. But Rogett shifted uncomfortably in his rocker. He had gotten more than a million of what he owned from his father. His host had inherited nothing, as far as he had learned, but information on how to handle a Colt, ride a horse and tell when one was being told the truth or a lie. Which, ruefully admitting to himself, Rogett could not do without an exhaustive investigation by Birnim & Birnim, his lawyers with offices near the Common.

And then suddenly, after such a long silence that Rogett felt himself slighted, his host began to talk. This was so surprising that Rogett hunched forward. "I beg your pardon—?"

Chapter Two

"I HAD ANOTHER NAME in those days," Kantrell said. "Never mind what it was. It was one of those tags people put on a man."

Rogett's host sat down in the rocker and stared at the hills.

"Er—what days, Mister Kantrell?" Rogett asked politely.

"Back before the war of the states. I wasn't nothing but a hard-tailed squirt with a fast gun and restless eyes and even more restless itch in my feet. I chose that way after paw whupped me the last time."

There was another long silence. "My paw was a tall drink of water that could ride a boar hog, if he had to. And the meanest man in the world when he was drunk, which was often. But the hardest-working old coot, and the kindest, gentlest man in the world with my maw and us kids when he wasn't."

"Er—wasn't what?"

"Drunk."

"Oh."

"I come from the Red Hill country back east of the forked Platte. Paw had a little place that us kids used to scratch around on trying to raise a little feed for ourselves and punch a few cattle—" Kantrell laughed shortly—"though I wouldn't have paw's cattle on my place now. Not even as butcher beef for the hands. They'd up and quit if I handed over cows like my paw had." He laughed again, a short, dry chuckle.

"Your father must have been one of the earliest settlers

in that part of the country," Rogett prompted. He was being polite again. He prided himself in an ability to guide a negligent conversation into the lines that he wanted. And he wished now that he had not only stoutly refused to remain overnight, but had refrained from inquiring about the quaint saying—*something—something—Jezebel.*

"Yup, paw was a man in the fur trade in the Rocky Mountains and worked for old John Jacob Astor's company for a while, then he hooked up with an outfit that Jim Bridger was with and trapped beaver with him. Paw was proud of being associated with old Jim. And then, as the beaver began to peter out and the market went dead with a change in styles, you might say, and less people hankering for beaver, it was already late in the eighteen-forties, but before the gold strike at Sutter's Mill over in California. Maw began to raise hell with him to come home and do his honorable duty to her and the kids—of which, Mistuh Rogett, there was eleven, with me the youngest."

"Oh, my God," Rogett groaned.

"Wasn't so bad. Only thing wrong was, that the whole time paw was home, he was always arguing with maw, claiming if she had let him go to California, he would have made his fortune."

Kantrell was silent again, smoking, puffing the cigar cherry red. "He might have, too. Paw was a toughern, and he jest might have done it."

"Strike gold?"

"Naw—mules and horses. Packing for the miners."

"Oh." Rogett considered that. Transport and supply to and from and area where neither of these items were available. A simple law in economics. Take it from where it is, and sell it at a high profit at a place where it isn't. The soundness of the basic principle of supply and demand appealed to the Bostonian. "So, remaining with your mother, he failed."

"Died a drunkard in a back alley fight over a painted woman," Kantrell said. "But I didn't see it. Like I said, I hightailed it away from home after the last time he took stovewood to me."

"How old were you, Mister Kantrell?"

"Eleven. Just turned eleven."

Rogett covered his face. When he was eleven, he remembered clearly, they had allowed him to ride alone in the park. "What on earth did you do?"

"First off—I lived with some Cheyenne for about two years and growed a little more. I ate regularly and worked —they fed me well, them Cheyenne, but they also worked the tail off'n me. But I learned from 'em. I learned a lot. Still using things I learned from them injuns. Finest goddamn men that walked the face of this earth." Kantrell laughed again, the short chuckle that Rogett had heard so often. "Folks around here talk about how tough the Apache—and the Ute and the Texas Comanche are—but by God, I'd put my sack of dust on a full-blood Cheyenne brave, on a Kansas broomtail, a Nec Perce double curved bow and war ax any time."

"They sound—superior."

"The brave that took me in was six feet six inches tall and weighed over two hundred twenty pounds—and he looked skinny. I seen him run a deer down barefooted and slam home his gut knife."

"That's a little incredible," Rogett said.

"I sent enough deer meat to boiling over a stick fire to know it's the truth. And I seen him do it with my own eyes."

"I wasn't—doubting your word, Mister Kantrell, but deer are notoriously—swift."

"Them goddamn Cheyenne was swifter," Kantrell said. Then he turned slowly, a sly look in his eyes. "You could probably confused me about your Boston, Mistuh Rogett. It's turn about."

Rogett grinned. It was the one outstanding trait he admired in the people he had met in the American West. They were just.

Kantrell moved his right hand to his side and there was a blur of motion, an explosion of noise and crashing of ricochet screams as Kantrell emptied his Colt, hitting six successive stones in the gate post a hundred feet away.

11

"Then, after drifting around until I was fifteen doing one thing or another, I stole this friend of mine from a drunken wrangler pushing cattle up to grass in Montana." He patted the smooth old gun affectionately.

Rogett's ears were still ringing, his eyes still not sure they had seen the fluid motion of the man's movements.

"I was fifteen when the first man tried to take it away from me, saying I was too young to have a gun. I shot his eyeballs out. I been shooting at eyeballs ever since. Though I ain't had to have a shoot-out in some time now. I got me a ramrod and overseer that does right well with an iron and when trouble comes. Bet goes out and fronts for me. You can do that without a loss of face in this country—when you got my reputation." He smiled. "Bet's a good man."

Rogett was astounded. "You've murdered—?"

"They always had a draw, Mistuh Rogett. Always."

"I see." Rogett could not resist asking, "You mentioned earlier you had another name."

"Yup. That goes along with the reputation. They called me Kid Kantrell."

"Kid Kantrell," Rogett repeated.

A soft-voiced woman appeared in the doorway behind them speaking in musical Spanish. Kantrell replied fluently and sat up. "Time to eat, Mistuh Rogett."

"What did you do after you murd— I beg your pardon—I mean, defended yourself against the man that tried to take your gun?"

Kantrell had moved ahead of his guest quickly and Rogett was not sure he had heard his question. They were entering the high-ceilinged living room that was nearly as large as the whole downstairs floor of the Bostonian's bachelor home in the East, and then into the dining room that was only a little smaller. "Bloody beef and biscuits" turned out to be one of the finest laden tables Rogett had ever seen. There were several different kinds of fowl, a full suckling pig, and a leg of roast beef that Rogett estimated must weigh at least seventy-five pounds. There were pots of rice, potatoes, beans, fried chicken on a huge

12

plate, and around the table, fourteen chairs, with a small side table for another ten, equally loaded down with food.

At first Rogett wondered if this was all for himself and Kantrell, having sensed that he was the only guest at the Kantrell Ranch. But he did not wonder long. A side door opened and there entered nearly two dozen of the roughest, dirtiest, foulest-smelling men Rogett had ever seen. They still wore their chaps and spurs and a few of them wore their guns. They filled the two tables and waited for Kantrell and Rogett to sit down. Each man had a greeting for the ranch owner. No one began to eat until a prolonged, inaudible and mumbled Grace was said by the little man seated at the head of the larger table. When they did begin, they went after the food with an enthusiasm that made the Easterner's eyes bulge.

"To answer your question, Mistuh Rogett, I came to this part of the country right after that incident, and met Jezebel."

The effect of that statement on the diners was amazing. The two tables had been full of soft laughter, conversation and jokes back and forth. Now it became absolutely silent. No one said a word, except to have something passed to them. They ate with their heads down, stuffing their mouths with food and washing it down with the steaming black coffee. This strange quiet that hovered over the table at the mention of Jezebel lasted throughout the meal. And then one by one, the men got up, turning with a brief nod toward Kantrell and Rogett, excusing themselves. The master of the house entertained his guest with silence. Not a word passed between them during the meal. Kantrell hunched over his food and ate with his fingers, digging into the flesh of a chicken with his forefinger, and drinking vast quantities of hot black coffee that was poured by the Spanish woman who hovered near his elbow.

When it was evident to Rogett that Kantrell was not going to indulge in dinner conversation, he fell to eating and found it difficult not to stuff himself. He managed a little restraint, remembering his occasional attacks of indigestion.

13

The meal, evidently, was over when Kantrell stood up and belched, shoved his chair to one side and disappeared through a door.

Rogett was left alone, except for the Spanish woman who waited patiently, coffee pot ready.

Chapter Three

SIDNEY ROGETT was nearing thirty-five. He was solidly
built, though a little heavy around the middle since he had
given up his daily rides in the park. He was considered
handsome, and he rode extremely well, something that had
pleased him a great deal when Kantrell and he had ridden
out to the hills to inspect the mine area. He had detected
the faintest gleam of amusement in the ranch owner's eyes
as Rogett had approached his horse and saw the look of
appreciation when the spirited animal acted up and Rogett
had to control him. He was firmly established in Boston's
social and financial upper circles by his name, which was
old and respected in New England, and by his own abil-
ities. Many had been pleased to see him double his in-
heritance in ten years; many more had doubted that he
would do anything but run through the money his father
had left him as soon as it was put into his hands.

One of those who hoped Sidney Rogett would settle
down and become an important, or at least a substantial,
member of Boston society was a girl he had known most
of his life and that he would eventually marry. Rogett
loved children and had decided on a quick settlement between himself and the young lady as soon as he returned
from his Western trip. He pulled out the latest letter from
Antonia and started to re-read it, his feet propped up on
one of the dining room chairs, puffing one of Kantrell's
really excellent cigars.

But he could not focus on the words. He folded the letter

and put it away. He smiled at the waiting Spanish woman, and walked through the living room to the veranda and sat down on the railing. He was not annoyed, exactly, at Kantrell's behavior, leaving him alone in the dining room without so much as a word, but he was piqued that the man had started a story about the damned Jezebel business and failed to continue. That—and the strange reaction of the men to the name, had aroused his curiosity.

There was a movement beyond the edge of the veranda. Rogett straightened up, and then the huge, brawny figure of Bet Jack Queen, made even larger by the heels and wide flap of his batwing chaps and heavy armor of web belt and Colt, mounted the steps of the house. "Evening, Mistuh Rogett," he said.

Sidney Rogett had met the man only briefly several days before when he had arrived on the stage and was a little surprised at the casualness in Queen's manner as he sat down, removing his hat and dropping it to the floor. "Fine night," Queen said.

"Lovely."

"Mistuh Kantrell—he usually takes a nap after eating. I thought I'd come over and sorta explain. I seen the look on your face when he upped and left you flat."

"Oh," Rogett said a little stiffly. "Thank you. I was about to retire myself." Rogett removed a leg from the railing.

"Don't run on my part. Stay and sit a while."

The man's manner was warm and there was no trace of the mockery in his voice that he could detect occasionally in Kantrell's, but then Kantrell was a millionaire and this man merely a hired man. "Thank you," Rogett said.

"Purty music, ain't it?" Queen remarked as the notes of a thonging Jew's-harp drifted up to them from the bunkhouse. "That's Skunk. He can play hell out of that thing when he wants to. Can't always get him to, though. Won't play when you ask him, only when he wants to play." Queen laughed softly.

"You all set up to start mining?" Queen asked after they listened to the end of the melody.

16

"Yes. We should start operations next spring."

"Good luck to you. Though I can't see much there to dig for."

"We know there's gold there," Rogett said, his voice just a little sharp. He did not like the inference that he was wasting money, or worse, didn't know what he was doing.

"I guess you do, if you put up half a million dollars to get the rights," Queen said.

"How did you know the terms?" Rogett demanded.

"I know everything," Queen said easily. "I'm not only ramrod, I'm general manager. It was me that took your company over the others that wanted to get in here."

"I didn't know there were others interested," Rogett said, his interest in the big man with the slow drawl increasing.

"Jest five. Not including you. I decided since you was your own boss, and had your own money to invest, and had made a killing or two back in the East, you would be easier to do business with than some company that's got a bunch of damn board members to argue out something that needs deciding right away."

Rogett warmed up a little. "I'm pleased that you like the way I handle my affairs, Mister Queen."

"Call me Bet. Everybody else does."

"Strange name," Rogett said.

"Yup. Family name of Queen, and Jack is after an uncle, and then the Bet comes from a brother that couldn't keep away from poker games. Used to have to take care of me, and every time he got a spare dime, he would be in some kind of a game, betting, always betting."

"Why call you Bet, if it was your brother that gambled?"

"That was the first word I learned. Bet."

Rogett laughed.

"How long have you been working for Mister Kantrell?"

"Not too long. About ten years. I drifted in from Texas and took on with him as top gun when he was trying to settle this valley."

"Were you around—when this Jezebel—was here?"

17

Rogett asked, and found himself breathing rapidly.

"How much did Mister Kantrell tell you?" Queen demanded.

"He was explaining the local saying, something about when it gets hot, Jezebel is throwing a fit in hell."

"That's the saying, all right," Queen replied.

"And the other one about a treasure of Aahasi."

"Yup. They go together," Queen said.

"Then you didn't know this Jezebel?" Rogett asked.

"Never saw her," Queen replied. "But you better ask your questions from the boss." And there was a sharp edge of command and authority in the ramrod's voice.

"Perhaps I will," Rogett said.

Queen stood up. He towered above Rogett by six inches. "Well, got to take a look at some stock over on the northwest line in the morning, better hit the hay. Goodnight, Mistuh Rogett."

Rogett accepted the offered hand and found that his own was lost inside the huge paw of the Westerner. He watched as the man walked down the steps and disappeared into the darkness with the hobbling grace, slightly bent at the knee, caused by the heels in soft ground, that all of them seemed to have.

He lingered on the veranda until he had finished the cigar and then turned toward the door. A good night's sleep and then the stage to Santa Fe tomorrow morning. He was tired. Perhaps it had been wise to remain for the night and get a good night's rest before the long overland journey.

He stepped into the living room—and stopped dead in his tracks. A girl was standing in the middle of the room staring at him. "Oh—I'm sorry," Rogett mumbled. He found himself staring. The woman in front of him was one of the most beautiful he had ever seen. She did not move. She stood tall, and her hair, pulled back from her face and hanging in a single rope down her back, was as black as ebony. She wore a white cotton blouse that revealed a white shoulder curving to the full bosom that the loose-

18

fitting blouse could not disguise. Her skirt was tan buck-skin and clung to her hips and thighs. And one spot of color: her lips. A deep, deep burgundy red. Her eyes were hot upon him.

"Who are you?" she demanded in a tight voice.

"Sidney Rogett—" he nodded his head slightly.

"What are you doing here?"

"Why— I—"

"Are you a doctor?"

"No. I'm a business associate of Mister Kantrell."

Rogett saw her relax, but the strain in her voice and the tension of her eyes held. "Just business?"

"Just business," Rogett assured her.

"Good night," she said suddenly and turned away.

"Just a minute—" Rogett took a half step after her.

"Yes?"

"May I ask who you are?"

"You don't know?"

"I'm afraid I haven't had the pleasure," Rogett said. She did not reply right away, but stared at him. Rogett found himself staring again. "Are you—" he asked, surprised to hear himself asking the question—"are you Jezebel?"

There was a movement in back of him. He turned and saw the Spanish woman enter the room. When he turned back, the girl was gone. The Spanish woman began to work around the room and then started for the door. "Just a moment!" Rogett said.

"Señor?"

"Do you understand English?"

"A leetle beet, Señor."

"That girl—here—a moment ago when you came in. Who is she?"

"Girl?"

"The señorita—!" Rogett insisted, and then heard himself. What difference did it make? "Who is she?"

"That is Miss Tasi Kantrell, señor."

"Not Jezebel?"

The woman's eyes became afraid. She tore herself free

19

and hurried through the dining room. Just before she pushed through the door leading to the kitchen, she threw a frightened glance back at Rogett.

Rogett was in his room. He had removed his coat and was sitting on the side of the bed about to remove his boots when the door opened and Bet Jack Queen, still wearing chaps and Colt, stepped inside.

"Don't Westerners usually knock before they enter a room?"

"Not if the room is full of nosey people," Queen said.

"I'm not sure I like that, Queen."

"I don't intend for you to. I told you don't ask no question unless you ask the boss. You went right inside and grabbed the Spanish woman."

"What is this!" Rogett demanded, standing up.

"Don't get riled, Mister Rogett." Queen stepped inside the room and closed the door. "Go on to bed and forget about everything."

"You can't threaten me," Rogett said suddenly, finding his voice. "And I don't like the way you try."

"There ain't," Queen said in a deliberate drawl, "a hell of a lot you can do about it, Rogett." He was standing away from the door, hands loose at his sides.

"Top gun," Rogett said. "That means what? Top killer, too?"

"Never you mind what it means. Just get your lily-white tail in that bed and keep it there until I personally put you on the Santa Fe stage tomorrow."

"Where is Mister Kantrell? I demand to see him at once."

"You may be a big man, and I reckon you are, back in Boston. And if I came to your part of the country, you could push me around. But you're in my country now, and I'm doing the pushing."

"You wouldn't dare draw that gun on me," Rogett said arrogantly and stepped forward.

"I won't need to—" Queen started to swing, and then stopped at the tattoo of hoof beats breaking out suddenly

20

in the stillness of the night. They faded rapidly, but had hardly started when the big cowboy let go of Rogett's shirt and ran down the hall to the large door at the end. He pounded on the door. "Mister Kantrell! Mister Kantrell!" He pushed the door open and entered, closing it after him.

Rogett, his face burning, stepped back into his room and closed the door. He walked to his valise and removed an over-and-under two-shot Derringer. He shoved it in his pocket, slipped on his coat and walked back to the door. He opened it in time to see Kantrell buckling on his gun-belt.

He hurried down the stairs and onto the veranda. In the distance he could hear voices and the low cursing of a man who is finding it difficult to move around in the darkness. There was much confusion, over what Rogett could not guess, and then he understood when he heard two dozen horses pound out of the stable area and ride hard into the night, in a direction Rogett knew to be toward the low hills and the mine area.

To hell with them! Rogett thought in a burst of rare temper. A host that ignores you after insisting you remain overnight. A hired hand who claims to be a general manager of a five million dollar ranch operation, but looks and acts like the admitted gunman he is, who threatens you with violence for asking a question. And what a question! Goddamn all of them and their superstitious fears, or real fears, or whatever. And then there was the strange young girl who asked you if you were a doctor and was surprised when you didn't know that she was Kantrell's daughter. A Spanish cook that is scared to death. Not to mention the hired hands that shut up like clams on a Cape Cod beach at the mention of a woman named Jezebel.

Rogett made his decision. He would pack his bags, borrow a horse and leave immediately. He would spend the night in a hotel in Jicarilla.

Stepping off the porch, he hurried to the bunkhouse. The huge room was empty. Beds unmade and things scat-

21

tered on the floor. Ample evidence of the haste the men made to ride out of the ranch stable into the dark night. Hell with them! He could saddle his own horse.

He walked down to the stables and opened the door. He found an old saddle, picked out a sturdy-looking sorrel and began to saddle up. He was cinching the animal when the door opened behind him and a man stood in the doorway.

"I wouldn't take that horse, mister," the man said.

Chapter Four

"ARE YOU GOING TO try and stop me?" Rogett demanded.

"Not too hard." The man was old. And when he moved in toward Rogett, the Easterner could see he limped. In the lamplight, as the man grew more distinct, Rogett saw that he was a grizzled, grey-bearded range veteran. He carried no gun. "What'cha wanta ride out in the dark for?"

"None of your business," Rogett said and turned back to cinching the saddle.

"You that Boston feller that come out to see about the mine in the hills, ain't you?"

"Yes."

"You don't know anything about this country, do you?"

"Enough to know that if I don't get out of it soon, I'll end up like the rest of you," Rogett said sarcastically. "Which to my mind leaves much to be desired."

"You're a pretty damn fancy talker, ain't you?" The old man laughed. "Used to know a feller talked like you. Sunday school teacher. Used to sweet-talk everybody in town, this was back in Texas, and everybody jest loved plumb hell out of him, until they found out he was sweet-talking the young women in town. That yummy-mouthed bastid would sweet-talk the drawers off'n any woman came along. Married, not married, maw or grandmaw! By God! They say that feller got some of everything they was in Lane County!"

Rogett pulled the horse out of the stall and started to lead him out of the stable. "They found out about him,

23

though. He got to sweet-talking two or three of them at one time. And it was the women that got a holt of him finally. They shore gave him a bruise!"

Rogett swung into the saddle and rode back to the main house that was dark and heavy against the night sky.

The old man walked after him and was holding the leather of the animal when Rogett came down the stairs holding his valise. "Yew don't want to go out there, mister," the old man said.

"I'm going."

"Yew ain't even got a gun."

"I have. And why would I need one?" Rogett showed him the double-barreled Derringer.

The old man cursed. "That thing a gun! Why them goddamn Apaches out there will pick their teeth on whatever lead that thing would throw."

"Don't try to fool me, old man," Rogett said. "I haven't seen an Indian since I've been here."

"No, dammit, and you ain't likely to, either! Why'n hell you think everybody went riding the hell out of here after Miss Tasi? 'Cause old Meathead's been seen messing around some of Mistuh Kantrell's beef."

"Meathead?"

"That's what we call him. A tough old cocker—like me—come from 'way back with Cochise and about the toughest Injun left in New Mexico. I never heard him called anything but Meathead."

"I don't believe you," Rogett said. He wheeled the horse around and started off into the dark. "Tell Mister Kantrell I found his hospitality unavoidably repugnant," Rogett yelled back at the old man.

"I couldn't remember that if you was to write it down on paper! You sure remind me of that feller back in Lane County," the old man yelled. "Tell him yerself, you'll be back!"

Rogett turned to look back at the old man walking back toward the bunkhouse and then spurred the horse into a trot.

He had gotten no more than two miles from the Kantrell ranch and was feeling very satisfied with himself for taking the initiative and leaving, when he heard the slight rustle of movement to his right.

Stopping the horse, Rogett pulled out the Derringer and waited. He heard the noise again, and then smiled as a small calf pushed through the brush on the side of the boulder-lined trail and, giving Rogett a passing look, continued down the trail toward the ranch.

Rogett slapped the horse gently on the flank and the animal moved ahead. The moon would be out soon, Rogett knew, because along with his interest in sailing ships on the East Coast, he had always spent a portion of his spare time studying the movements of the celestial bodies. As soon as the moon ventured out from behind the clouds, it would be easy for him to see the trail ahead.

He rode for another twenty minutes, enjoying the feeling of being alone in the wilderness; it was the first time that he had actually felt the presence of the wildness of the West, since he had always been in the company either of Kantrell or some of his men when they had inspected the mine sites.

He thought of Antonia, and of the evening they would spend together while he told her of the details of his trip. He would tell her about this ride, solitary and certainly far from warlike, from the Kantrell ranch to Jicarilla while Meathead was supposed to be lurking about.

The thought of the Apache made the man take a tighter grip on the leather with his left hand, while holding the Derringer with his right.

Sidney Rogett possessed a brand of courage that is part arrogance and part confidence, both of these personal attitudes a result of his life in the ready, well-heeled and able society of Boston. Courage and bravery were intwined with honor. And while Rogett might not have been conscious of his arrogance, or his courage, he would certainly have responded to any assault on his honor, and in the end produced a ferocious foe, absolutely unafraid.

25

So, when Rogett took a tighter grip on his two-shot Derringer, it was with a steady hand. He urged his horse up the trail, eyes and ears alert for any movement or sound in the night. And he did not panic when the arrow whistled by his head, burying itself into the trunk of a half-dead tree.

Rogett slipped off the sorrel and moved into the nearest pool of shadows and waited. The horse remained perfectly still, having been trained to stay where he was when the rider dismounted.

Rogett listened. He was not frightened, but he was cautious. He had made an error in judgment, due to his rancor toward Kantrell and Queen, of the old man in the stable. He should have listened to him, and Rogett was perfectly willing to admit his mistake and return to the security of Kantrell's big house. But at the moment, he remained still and waited for the other to show his position.

He did not wait long. He saw the Indian move at the top of a boulder on the far side of the trail. He raised the little gun and took a careful aim. He fired. The Indian slumped forward.

There was a sudden sound beyond the fallen Indian. Another head appeared in exactly the same spot as the first. Rogett took aim again, firing, killing the second Indian as cleanly as the first. There was a clatter of hooves beyond the boulder where Rogett could see the fallen bodies of the two Indians. The hoofbeats faded into the night.

Rogett moved slowly out of his protective hiding place and advanced toward the horse. The animal did not move. He remained perfectly still, ready to swing into the saddle and retreat back to the Kantrell house at the slightest warning, but he was reasonably sure there wasn't anything else to be afraid of. After five minutes, he probed the opposite side of the rocky trail and climbed to the boulder. The Indians were quite dead, with bullet holes in their foreheads. They carried bows, sheaths of arrows and carbines. Both of them were young. Rogett guessed in the dim light they might be in their early twenties.

And then the realization that he had killed—not one—but two human beings, settled his fears. He made sure they were dead, vaguely hoping that they might not be so that the incredible act would be removed from his conscience.

The full weight of death—at his own hand—descended on him slowly but with a clap of thunder. They were *dead!*

Skunk was playing the Jew's-harp when Rogett returned to the stable, the bodies of the two Indians slung across the back of the sorrel.

"Yippeee!" Skunk danced and clapped his hands at the sight of the two neat holes in the Apaches' heads. "Mistuh, you done skint it now."

"They attacked me," Rogett said coldly.

"Yeah—but you kilt old Meathead's *son!*" Skunk cried, "He's going tear this place to hell fer this I reckon! Hot damn, there's going to be shooting and killing jest like it was in the old days." The old man turned to the bunkhouse. "Better git my old carbine ready—" he said, with high excitement in his voice.

"Come back here!" Rogett demanded. The old man stopped. "Come here and help me with these—bodies."

"We gotta git ready, mistuh, 'cause sure as hell, old Meathead is going to come raising hell down here—"

"Never mind that. Help me get these bodies down and into the stable," Rogett commanded, and in his voice old Skunk recognized the whip of authority.

Skunk limped back to the sorrel and awkwardly, breathing hard, stumbling in the dark, they removed the two Indians and laid them side by side in the stable. Rogett began to remove the leather from the sorrel while the old man examined the two carbines, the bows and the sheaths of arrows.

When they were finished, the old man implored Rogett to take the guns and hurry to the main house. "They're gonna come down in here, Mistuh Rogett, and they gonna be after hair. It might be hours before Betajack and Mistuh Kantrell come back. That Miss Tasi can ride good as any

27

man and she's on the Prince."

"Prince?"

"A big brown streak of lightening of a stallion. They might have to go all the way to the buffalo waller before they catch up with her," Skunk said. And considering that he had not listened to the old man about leaving the house and trying to reach Jicarilla, Rogett decided to take his advice.

"How many are in the house?" Rogett asked as they took the carbines belonging to the Indians and hurried to the veranda. "Anyone beside the Spanish woman?"

"Her husband. The cook. Name's Juan. But he's oldern I am and sick in bed," Skunk said.

"We'll keep it quiet then," Rogett decided. "No use having them up and around and exciting them unless Meathead actually attacks."

"Reckon that's all right. But if he does come, she can load for us." Rogett could not help but grin at the enthusiasm Skunk could not hide at the prospect of a fight.

They hurried into the house and closed the shutters that were made of heavy red wood and laced with gun holes. With the house shuttered, the lights out and the moon just rising, they could see the whole front area of the house-yard, and the little road that lead to the Jicarilla trail.

Chapter Five

THEY HAD SETTLED themselves before the two largest windows that flanked the main door. Each man had two carbines, shells, a Colt, and Skunk had found a double-barreled shotgun. "Ain't nothin' like scatter shot when a bunch of 'em rush at you," he had told Rogett, his voice and manner excited as he limped back to the window.

They had been sitting for an hour in silence, watching the moon rise, and had seen no sign of Meathead or his braves. Rogett was beginning to think that perhaps the old man's imagination had run away with him, carrying Rogett along with it, when a second hour had passed and there was still no sign of the Indians. "Who is Jezebel?" Rogett asked suddenly.

Skunk made a funny noise in his throat. "Mist' Rogett, don't shoot straight questions like that at me without no slow buildup."

"I'm sorry. But too much has been made of it since I've been here." He talked slowly, telling the old man of the silence on the subject by Kantrell, the visit by Queen, the sudden appearance of Tasi, the old Spanish woman's fear and the unusual behavior of the men when the subject was brought up at the table.

Skunk did not answer for a while. "Don't," he said with a distinct plea in his voice, "go digging into Jezebel, Mist' Rogett. It's—a funny business."

"But you know something, don't you?" Rogett pressed.

"No more than the gossip in the saloons in town, or any more than most people know around here."

29

"I don't even know that much," Rogett said.

"Then you going to have to find out someplace else. I got me a good thing in this place. I'm too old to get out and scatter around the country trying to make a living. I don't have nothing to do but take care of the horses and the stable, and that's all right with me, cause I like horses and I like the smell of stables." Skunk hesitated. "I don't want Betajack throwing me out."

"Then tell me this much. Why did Tasi think I might be a doctor?" Rogett asked.

"She asked you that?" Skunk's voice was sharp.

"Yes. And she seemed surprised that I didn't know who she was," Rogett replied.

"Look, Mistuh Rogett, maybe we better do less talking and more watching for Meathead and his bunch—" Skunk said, trying to avoid the subject.

"Meathead isn't coming and you know it," Rogett said sharply.

"Well, he might."

"Why would a top gun, as he described himself to me, like Queen, be a general manager of Kantrell's ranch?"

" 'Cause he's damn good at cattle."

"You won't talk, eh, Skunk?" Rogett said. "Very well, I'm afraid I'll have to tell Queen that you sent me into town with tall tales of an Indian attack coming, and used it all as an excuse to get inside Mister Kantrell's liquor."

The old man laughed. "How you going to explain them dead Injuns out in the stable?"

"No explanation necessary. They attacked me—as they really did—but that doesn't make any difference to your sending me out alone in the night when you knew I didn't have much of a chance."

"But I didn't say that! I tried to get you from going!"

"But Queen will believe me, Skunk."

The old man fell silent again. Rogett could hear him mumbling to himself. "Was Kantrell married to Jezebel?"

"Yeah. He was married to her," Skunk said.

"And Tasi is their daughter?"

"Yeah—in a way—I guess so."

30

"What do you mean, in a way?"

"Dammit, Mist' Rogett, ain't you got any sense of justice? You could get me fired, if Queen knew I was talking about—"

"No one will know, Skunk. I give you my word," Rogett said.

"You do?" Skunk asked almost childishly. "You promise?"

"Promise," Rogett said, his eyes sweeping the moonlight-flooded area beyond the veranda. "What do you mean, Tasi is Kantrell's daughter 'in a way'?"

"She's Aahasi's child."

"Aahasi? You mean the one mentioned in the saying about the treasure?"

"Yup. Jezebel was the mos' beautiful woman I ever saw in my whole life," Skunk said. "Looked a lot like Miss Tasi, but prettier in every way. And there was a lot of the wildness in her that Tasi has—ridin' off in the dark and all that."

Skunk sat back from his crouching position before the window and Rogett could hear him drinking heavily from the bottle of liquor the old stable man had taken out almost as soon as he had taken the guns to defend himself. "I was working for the biggest outfit in these parts then—"

"When was this?"

"Back about twenty-five years ago. It was a wild, mean goddamn country. Choose any square mile and you'd find fifty different things ready to kill you. Mean goddamn country. Cochise was a big man then. Used to give the Army fits and Saturday night trots. Take a dozen of his Injuns and slam down hard on a whole damn double troop of soljers and give 'em hell. Then ride off and lose hisself in the rocks."

"When did you first see Jezebel?" Rogett asked.

"Soon as she hit Jicarilla. She came in on the supply train from Santa Fe, wearing pants like a man and toting a hand gun she could shoot better'n most. They wasn't a goddamn ounce of woman ninny in her. She marches in to the saloon and sits down in the corner and starts a poker game. Four days later, she owned that goddamn saloon—

31

and that's a fact—and took off her man's pants and put on a dress. It was like a party in a king's castle the night she opened up the Jezebel Saloon. She brought in women from Santa Fe and California, and she had 'em fixed up like fairy queens, Mist' Rogett. And Jezebel was the mother of 'em all. That was the night she shot Concho in a shoot-out. Concho owned the saloon before she gambled him out of it and he came in that night drunked up, and started blowing about how he was going to take it back and she had cheated him in cards. Damn if she didn't sober him up with coffee and then strap on a hand gun and straighten him out. Put two leads in his heart in a two-inch circle, fanned that old gun, mind, and then took the gun off, and went back to making people feel at home in her saloon.

"It was soon after that, that Kantrell came to town with a reputation and a gun. They seemed to click it off right away. Miss Jezebel would call the tune and Kantrell would back it up with that gun." Skunk took another long swallow of Kantrell's private liquor and was quiet until Rogett prompted him with a question.

"How did they get along?"

"Hard to describe. I heard 'em fight more'n once. Over little things. He didn't like her to play poker at the tables with the men, and she told him to mind his own business. Now, they was several people in town that didn't like either one of them and tried to separate 'em, got in between them, know what I mean?"

"Divide and conquer."

"That's it. Damn if you don't remind me of that feller in Lane County. Said he got some of everything they was to be had."

"Was anyone successful in their attempts to come between them?"

"Hell, no! Soon as anyone would start anything, they'd get together and be close as hell and fight it down."

"What kind of things would they fight down?"

"You name it, Mist' Rogett, and Miss Jezebel and Kantrell was in on it."

"All of it legal?"

32

"Not a damn bit of it legal. Everything you could think of that was against the law and that ought to bring in money, that was what they was in. From rustling cattle, to stealing land, making deals with Cochise and then breaking them off, then doing the same thing with the Army. They took gold mines from people, and when the people objected, they shot the people down like rattlesnakes. At least Kid Kantrell did the shooting."

"How long did this unholy alliance last?" Rogett asked. He was resisting half of what the old man said, but there was the ring of truth in Skunk's way of telling it.

"Everything was fine until that Indian showed up."

"Aahasi?"

"That's him. Biggest, toughest-looking sonofabitch that ever rode a horse. Now you know Kantrell is a little man. Tough as all hell, ready to fight anytime, like most little men. They seem to carry a grudge against the whole world 'cause they feel they got cheated when God started handing out sizes. This Injun was just Kantrell's meat. Good-looking man, only one I ever saw in my life I'd say was pretty. Like a woman. No, not exactly, like some pitchurs I seen of them old-timey bastards that walked around in bedsheets in the Bible days."

"Romans?"

"That's them! Looked like one of them. With a big nose and a lot of hair that was black as coal and bright as the sun when he was outside. And lemme tell you something, that sonofabitch was big! With the biggest shoulders you'll ever hope to see on a man. And strong as a damned mule. He comes to Jicarilla—and says he's a Jicarilla Apache— that's where the town done got its name from—the Jicarilla Apache Indians—and says to the first man he sees, 'This town is mine. It belongs to the Jicarilla people.' Jest like that. I don't know who it was in town he spoke to, later some of us tried to find out, but we couldn't. Anyway, he must have been a funny feller, cause this feller ups and answers Aahasi. 'Then you better talk to Miss Jezebel, because damn if she don't *own* this town!' "

Rogett had not looked out into the moonlit yard for

some time now, wholly absorbed in the story Skunk was telling him.

"Did he go see her?"

"Right straight away. Marched into that saloon and lemme tell you, he made a powerful goddamn figure of a man when he steps inside. Stands there, feet apart, hands at his sides and glares at everybody. Then he bellows in pretty good English, 'This is Aahasi!' and he slaps his chest like an ape does. 'Who is woman who owns this town!' he bellows again. Well, by now, you kin jest imagine what that saloon was like. It got so quiet you could hear the dealer at the black jack table slipping an ace out of his bottom deck of burnt cards."

Skunk laughed, the slow skittering laugh of an old man in memory.

"Did she dare to come out?" Rogett asked.

"She wasn't afraid of nothing, I'm telling you. She comes over to him and—the closer she gets, the slower she's looking at him. This was one hell of a man and she knew it. 'I'm the woman you seek,' she says to him. 'What do you want?' Then the Kid walks in. Man, that was something. It looked like a mouse running around an elephant. He pushes Jezebel back and out the way and then steps around this big Injun like he was examining a horse, or a mule, or something. Then he goes back to the front of him. 'You walkin' or ridin'?' Kantrell asks him. The Indian don't move. He looks at the Kid like he don't even know what it is. 'You walkin' or ridin'?' the Kid asks again.

"The Indian don't even look at him again. He looks around the saloon and bellows again, and I mean *bellows*. Made the glasses shake in back of the bar. 'This Aahasi town! All people get out!' he says. And there was a few that was ready to pack their saddle bags and leave right now! But the Kid sees the look on Jezebel's face and won't stand for this much longer. He moves for his hand gun, and Mist' Rogett, I seen fast things in my life. Like the dart of a rattler, not any of these Mex snakes, but a big Texas rattler, eight feet long, and I seen a mountain cat go after an eagle once when it was a hard winter, and I seen men

34

who was fast with a gun. All of them couldn't match Kid Kantrell. But this goddamn Injun whips out an Apache knife *faster*. He slashes the Kid's gun hand—maybe you seen the scars on his hands?—and then makes a slash at his neck. Before the Kid knows what's happening, he's on the floor belly-aching and the blood pumping outa him like a spring well in Wyoming.

"Now by this time, Miss Jezebel is going into *her* dance! She grabs a hand gun from a stranger and levels at this big Indian's chest—but before she can cut loose, he's done flang that goddamn knife of his'n at her and it goes right through her shoulder. Miss Jezebel falls down, Aahasi looks to see if anyone else is asking for action that afternoon, but they wasn't. He goes over to Jezebel, picks her up and walks out with her. Kicking Kid Kantrell out of the way like he would a dead dog as he heads for the door."

"My God," Rogett found himself saying. "My God."

"Then he stops at the door and turns around. And he says it out plain as day: 'The treasure of Aahasi lingers yet for the one that will dig in the shadows before the sun rises,' then he walks on out of town, gets on his horse and rides into them hills yonder." Skunk pointed to the area where Rogett would place his mine. "And ain't nobody—*nobody*—seen hide or hair of them since that day."

"But—but—where did—Tasi come from?"

"Sent her down out of the hills one day when she was two, strapped to one of Kantrell's horses old Aahasi knew would find its way home."

"But how did they know it was Jezebel's—and Aahasi's child?" Rogett asked.

"The little thing was wearing a dress made out of the same stuff her maw was wearing when Aahasi took her away."

Rogett wiped his face and found that he had been sweating. "What did Kantrell do?"

"Well—first off—" Skunk was interrupted by the clatter of a troop of horses riding into the area. "Here comes Queen! Thank God for that! Yippeee!" Skunk got up and

35

hurriedly put Kantrell's bottle of liquor away and threw the door open.

Rogett stepped to the doorway just as Bet Jack Queen, Kantrell and Tasi entered. The girl looked at him wildly, and then passed through the door and made for the stairs. The four men stood in the doorway and watched her until her door was slammed closed.

Chapter Six

"WHAT THE HELL ARE YOU doing here?" Queen demanded of Skunk.

"Meathead—" Skunk began to explain.

"Just a minute, Skunk," Rogett said. "Mister Kantrell, there are a few things I would like to discuss with you—"

"I'm tired, Mistuh Rogett—" Kantrell said, Taking off his gun belt. "Whatever it is can wait until morning."

Bet Jack Queen smiled. "Looks like Skunk just hooted you into letting him at the boss's whiskey, Mister Rogett. We don't have any Indians around here—none that will bother you. As fer Meathead—"

Rogett's voice was hard and he clamped down on Queen's surly manner like a steel trap. "There are two dead Apaches in the stable. Both of them with holes in their heads that I put there on the way into Jicarilla. Skunk identified them as the son and another brave of this Meathead—and suggested we hole up inside the house in case of a reprisal attack, until you returned."

Before either Queen or Kantrell could speak, several men ran up onto the steps of the veranda and excitedly documented Rogett's statements. A moment later, one of the bodies, the one Skunk said was that of Meathead's son, was brought to the veranda.

Kantrell and Queen looked at each other, their eyes exchanging a look of what Rogett roughly guessed to be fear. They turned to examine the body. And while they were bending over in the lamplight, several of the hard men eyed Rogett speculatively, grinning, and one of them even

37

complimented him on his shooting. "Must be a dang buster when you can do that to a Meathead Apache in the dark, with a pea shooter."

"Take him back to the stable," Queen ordered the men. "Nobody sleeps. Keep the horses saddled and after you get coffee, check your guns. Meathead won't let this pass."

"You shouldn't have attempted to go into town alone," Kantrell said, trying hard to keep the irritation out of his voice when he spoke to Rogett. "This is a serious situation. Meatheat is a dangerous Indian. He has nearly a hundred renegade followers that will do anything to keep from living on a reservation. I've let them have all the beef they want from my herds. A double protection against rustlers and against the damage they could do if they wanted to," Kantrell said bitterly. "And you go riding out and kill his son!"

"I was attacked," Rogett replied coolly, not at all intimidated by Kantrell's manner or his words. "I was forced to leave your hospitality by the arrogant manner of this man—" and he pointed to Queen—"by this man who threatened me with violence if I asked any more questions about Jezebel."

The name exploded in the room like a bomb.

"Good night, Mister Rogett," Kantrell said abruptly. "I suggest you go to your room and remain there until I can safely conduct you to Jicarilla."

"The sooner you can arrange for any transportation out of this country, the more I will be indebted to you, sir," Rogett said. "Good night, Mister Skunk," he said to the old man.

"Good night, Mist' Rogett."

Rogett stopped at the bottom of the stairs and turned to face them. "I hope, Mister Kantrell, that you will not allow the personally strained relations between us to deprive this man, Mister Skunk, of his job. In all things tonight, he was perfectly proper and helpful, always looking after my welfare."

Kantrell nodded slightly. "I appreciate your consideration for this man."

"Damn if he ain't a fancy talker. Jest like that feller back in Lane County with them drawers-dropping women."

Rogett had settled himself, cleaning and re-loading his gun. He removed his boots, but otherwise remained dressed. He stretched out in the dark and listened to the men below his window as they prepared for an attack by Meathead.

He did not feel sleepy. He thought about shooting the two Indians and when the full realization of the streak of the arrow past his head came to him in the dark, he began to sweat.

There was a noise in his room. He hadn't been thinking about the shooting of Meathead's son. He had been dreaming, and the noise awoke him. Already, in the short time that he had been in this wild country, part of its habits and cautions were becoming his. When he heard the noise, he did not open his eyes. He remained perfectly still, his fingers gripping the handle of the little gun. Whoever it was moved toward the bed. He could hear the sharp breathing.

Rogett spun off the bed, dropped to his knees and brought up the gun. "Stand still," he commanded in a low voice.

The movement stopped.

"Light the lamp. And don't think I'll hesitate to shoot."

He heard the scraping of a match and then slowly the figure came alive out of the darkness. "Miss Tasi—!" Rogett gasped.

The girl was in rough-looking riding clothes. "I—"

Rogett went to her, putting the gun away. "What are you doing here?"

"You've got to help me!" she said. She turned to the window and pulled back the curtains carefully and stared down into the stable area.

"Help you?"

"You can get out of here—and you've got to take me with you!" The girl continued to watch the activity in the stable area. "You can get a horse—"

"Even if I knew what kind of trouble you're in, and knowing it, agreed that I should help you, I couldn't get a horse any easier than you. Or haven't you heard? Your father has asked—commanded—me to remain in this room until he can get me safely to town," Rogett said.

"Get Skunk. He'll help us. He's a friend," Tasi said. "Oh, please, Mister Rogett. You've got to help me!"

"I don't have to do anything," Rogett said coldly. Tasi spun away from the window. "Kantrell is not my father!" she said bitterly.

"That still doesn't help you get out of here."

"Oh, why won't you help me? Are you in with them?"

"I'm in with no one."

"If I leave this house, they'll tell Queen."

"Who are *they*?"

"The men. There isn't one of them that would dare help me—or dare not tell Queen if they saw me leave. Everyone of them is afraid of him."

"I'm afraid you're talking in riddles," Rogett replied. "I don't know what your problem is, Miss Tasi, and I can't honestly say that I want to know. I would like to help you but it appears that this is a family matter and I learned a long time back not to mix with family rows."

"Will you do one thing for me?"

"What is that?"

"Will you tell Skunk to fix a horse and have it out near the big boulder at the head of the Jicarilla Trail in an hour?"

"That might be impossible to do."

"No it won't. You can leave this room."

"Yes. I can leave the room. But why should I?"

"I could tell you—"

"Yes?"

"I'll make a business deal with you, Mister Rogett," Tasi said, her voice suddenly becoming a little calmer, a little more sure of herself. "I'll give you valuable information if you will tell Skunk to have that horse ready."

40

"What kind of information?"

"About your mining operations here."

"Mine operations?" Rogett studied her face. "What could you tell me about the mine that I don't know?" he said slowly, dropping into that Boston reserve that was like a wall of security around him when he was on unsafe ground.

"How much do you pay for the option rights to begin operations?"

Rogett hesitated. After all, Queen knew, and there wasn't any reason to believe that everyone didn't know. And what if they did? "I paid a half million and ten percent of what we take out of the ground," Rogett said.

"You can kiss that half million goodbye!" Tasi laughed shortly. "And as for the ten percent, you won't take ten cents worth of ore out of the hills."

Rogett stiffened. "But I have a contract."

"Sure you do. But there isn't anything in that contract that guarantees you access to the mine area."

"Access! Why—we rode over the entire area. Who would prevent us from working?" Rogett asked.

"My father," she said lightly.

"Kantrell? Why would he want to stop me?"

"Kantrell is not my father."

Rogett felt the skin tightening around his mouth. "Aahasi?"

"Aahasi," Tasi said. "Now, do you help me?"

Rogett laughed. "What you say is ridiculous. One man preventing a company from going into the hills."

"Aahasi is not an ordinary man," she said.

"Still—"

"*You will not take one bucket of ore out of that mountain!*"

"See here—if that happens—the contract is null and void," Rogett said.

"No, it isn't. I've heard them planning this a long time. Long before you came here, Mister Rogett. Why do you think they insisted that you remain overnight? Because they wanted time to deposit that check of yours."

"If I don't—" Rogett stopped. It was clear now, crystal clear. They had given him an option on land to mine ore—gold ore—knowing that it would be inaccessable. They had signed the contract—which had a premium date of mine operation beginnings of three years—and should he fail to start those operations within that three-year period—he would lose his money and the rights to the land. There had been no question about his beginning operations within three years. But if there was certain knowledge on their part that he would not start the operations it would make the five hundred thousand dollar deposit he had given Kantrell like money found in the street. And their behavior—Kantrell's insistence on his staying over—had given him time to put through a payment demand on the check.

But, Rogett's mind reeled, why did they take a chance on his staying behind to discover all this? Now that he knew, he could stop payment on the check and let them sue him for breach of contract.

"See here," Rogett demanded of Tasi. "Why are you so desperate to leave here? And why do you think they will stop you?"

"I can't tell you that now. If you'll help me—I'll tell you everything—"

There was a sudden harsh knock on the door. Kantrell's voice filled the room. "Tasi! Tasi, are you in there?"

Tasi looked at Rogett and the blood drained out of her face. Rogett set his teeth and stepped toward the door. He flung it open. Kantrell stood in the hallway, his face livid.

"I've killed men for a lot less than this, Rogett," Kantrell said in a voice that was just under control. "A lot less."

"And what do you think has happened, Mister Kantrell, that would provoke you to killing so indiscriminately?"

Kantrell did not answer. He looked at Tasi and snapped his fingers. He jerked his head. There was no mistaking his meaning for Tasi to leave. She did not

42

move. Rogett noticed the open, undisguised hatred Tasi felt for the man at the door. Slowly, and with great effort, Kantrell spoke when Tasi did not move. "This is not a very nice thing to do to your father."

"You're not my father!" Tasi said.

"Kantrell's eyes tightened. "Come along, daughter," he said quietly. "Don't make a move, Mister Rogett. Just because we've had business together, don't think I wouldn't hesitate to shoot. The only thing that has saved your life—" he stopped and swallowed hard—"until now is that she still has her clothes on."

"I'm sure my death wouldn't be hard to explain," Rogett said. "It would be easy enough—with Meathead running loose, wouldn't it?"

"Don't put ideas in my head," Kantrell commented softly. "Come along, Tasi."

She looked at Rogett desperately to signal him, and passed through the door. "I take it you're going to lock me in—like a sullen child being punished for naughtiness," Rogett said as sarcastically as he could.

"Won't be necessary. Just stay away from Tasi. Next time I see you with her alone, I'll kill you." Kantrell said dispassionately. Apparently, Rogett thought, he had regained control. Then quickly, Rogett wondered if Kantrell had heard Tasi speaking to him, telling him of the planned swindle.

"Oh, by the way—" Rogett said, trying to keep his voice under control and make it sound casual.

"Yes?"

"Since we have apparently run afoul of personality by-play in our relationship, I thought I had better warn you. The binding check I gave you—" He brought his eyes up level with Kantrell's. "It can't be cashed until I return to Boston. A little guarantee I arranged before I left. No Sidney Rogett—no half million dollar payment."

"I could consider that a breach of contract—"

"Just a little insurance against accidents."

Kantrell smiled confidently. "If I wanted to kill you, Mister Rogett, and make it look like an accident, no amount of insurance that you might have would stop me—"

"Oh, yes! Seen Aahasi lately? Pretty good man with a knife, I hear."

The smile vanished. The blood rushed into Kantrell's face. He dropped his hand and gripped the gun. "You got a nosey face."

"Remember—no Sidney Rogett in Boston—no half million dollars."

Kantrell kicked the door with his boot, slamming it hard.

Rogett decided he would wait ten minutes. He forced himself to sit on the side of the bed and wait the full time. It was still pitch dark outside, and it would not be dawn for another three hours. In the ten minutes, he studied the contract. The promise of Kantrell to lend all possible assistance in the mine operation, Rogett saw now, would stop short of armed protection, or armed help, in securing the mine area against Aahasi and Meathead. In fact, it would be easy enough to set Meathead and Aahasi—if there was a connection between the two Indians—against the mine operations by creating an incident of some sort to provoke the Indians into attacking. And the cost of sustaining an army of guards to protect the huge operation he had in mind for the project would be costly—not to mention dangerous.

But why was Kantrell so dead set against letting the girl leave? And why did she want to ride out of the Kantrell ranch in the middle of the night—when Meathead was prowling around? All right, Rogett thought, granted that Meathead is tied in with Aahasi in some way, wasn't she dressed up as a man? If the Apaches had attacked him in the dark on the road to Jicarilla without first making sure who he was, how would they know that the girl, dressed in men's clothes, was really Tasi, daughter of Aahasi?

It was too much for Rogett. He snapped himself up straight and walked the length of the room. Another two

44

minutes to wait before he could open the door. He made sure the two-shot gun was ready and continued to pace the floor. There was no chance of Kantrell missing out on his scheme to swindle the half million from Rogett unless he got away and stopped payment on the check. And now that he had warned Kantrell that the check would not be honored until his safe return to Boston, Kantrell might just decide to keep Rogett at the ranch until approval of the check was made. There wasn't a thing in the world, Rogett saw suddenly, to prevent the man from doing just that. And if he was clever enough to figure out the elaborate scheme to swindle a half million dollars, there wasn't any reason to believe that he wouldn't simply keep Rogett a prisoner until the check had been cashed.

He had to get away!

The odds seemed impossible, the gamble a useless one. There was Meathead lurking around, waiting for anyone to show his face in the unprotected land around the ranch, and there was Kantrell, Queen and his men.

The girl! Tasi could get him safely into Jicarilla, if he could get her past Kantrell and Queen's men.

There were many more questions that Rogett wanted to examine carefully, but there wasn't any time. The ten minutes had passed. He stepped to the door.

It was no problem to get to the bottom of the stairs. The house was dark and empty. Apparently Kantrell had gone to bed. But had he? And what had he done to Tasi when they left Rogett's room?

He slipped back up the stairs quickly and moved to the door he had seen Tasi enter when they had returned from their ride. He tried the door, pressing gently. It came open. He stepped inside. "Tasi?" he asked softly.

Silence.

"Tasi!" There was a rush of wind near his ear. He tried to avoid it, but the blow caught him on his neck in back of the ear. He tried to claw his way back to the vague light he saw flashing in his eyes from a long way

45

off. Then, he lost ground, and the light went out.

He struggled to his feet, pulling himself up against a chest of drawers. His head felt as if it were going to fall off. The back of his neck was so stiff he could hardly move his head, and this contradiction of feelings—the head that wanted to fall off, and the neck that wouldn't let it—lasted until he was on his feet and trying to focus.

The room was still dark. How long had he been unconscious? He pulled out his watch and studied it. My God! he thought. It had felt like an eternity, but actually it had been only three or four minutes.

"Tasi—?" he managed weakly. "Tasi, are you here?" Silence.

He decided to gamble on a match. He struck it and watched the yellow flame light the room, eyes probing quickly for some sign of the girl. The room was empty.

He dropped the match to the floor and turned to the door. He opened it carefully, in time to see Queen walking down the hall to Rogett's room, his Colt in his hand, with a grim expression on his face. He was walking on his toes. He watched while the ramrod threw open the door of his room. He reappeared a moment later, a puzzled look on his face. He hurried down the hall past Tasi's door. When he was a few feet past Rogett, the Bostonian slipped out behind the big man and pushed the Derringer into his back. "Just stand still, Queen." He removed the heavy Colt and stuck it in his waist. "Don't make the mistake of thinking that you can do anything. Remember the Apaches and the neat little holes in the middle of their heads. You bad men give me a pain in the neck with your exaggerations about gun shooting. If you want to see fancy shooting, Queen, just try to do something other than what I tell you."

"You haven't got a piss ant's chance, Rogett," Queen growled. "My men will take you the minute you top the first step on the veranda."

"No, they won't. They've got a healthy respect for me and my little pea shooter after the two Indians were stretched out in the stable."

Queen remained silent.

"Where's Miss Tasi?"

"You don't know?" Queen was genuinely surprised.

"I'm asking the questions, Queen."

"I don't know where she is. Kantrell sent me up here to see if she had slipped back into your room."

"I don't believe that. I think you came up here to get me and force me to come along with you on a ride on a dark trail where I might meet an accident."

"You got a lively imagination, Rogett."

"I got a livelier trigger finger, now move."

They walked down the stairs slowly, with Rogett ready and perfectly willing to shoot the man in the back of the head if he should threaten a move against him. "Open the door and tell the others everything is all right. Tell them to leave the horses where they are, you'll have Skunk take care of them, and for them to go back to bed. Tell them they'll need their sleep and tomorrow is going to be a tough day."

"They won't. They'll know something is wrong," Queen said.

"They better believe you, Queen. They better."

"I'll do my best."

"That's the spirit."

"Careful of that pea shooter," Queen said.

"Never mind the pea shooter," Rogett replied, "just do what I told you. And ask them if they've seen Miss Tasi—and Skunk."

"Skunk!"

"Move!"

Queen opened the door. A half dozen men waited near as many horses in front of the veranda steps and turned to look up at Queen and Rogett. "Tell 'em," Rogett insisted and rammed the gun in the cowboy's back.

Queen repeated what Rogett had ordered him to say and the men accepted it without a word of protest. They didn't exactly like the idea of riding out in the dark when Meathead was on the prowl.

"Any of you seen Miss Tasi?" Queen asked.

"Not since you been inside," one replied.

"How about Skunk?"

"He was messing around the stable—"

"Send him over here," Rogett hissed to Queen. And the Westerner repeated the order to the men. They hurried off in the darkness, not wanting to remain and have their ramrod change his mind. It had been a hell of a night and the idea of riding out again was a dim prospect. They were only too glad to be let off the hook.

"Now what?" Queen asked.

"Just move over to the railing and sit down easily. I'll sit here in Kantrell's rocker and wait for Skunk."

"I might try and run," Queen said.

"Go ahead," Rogett replied. "I could probably get you in the back of the head before you got ten feet."

"You're pretty damn cocky from what you were earlier this evening," Queen said, moving to the railing and showing no signs of trying to improve his position.

"You might say I was a different man."

"I doubt that."

"Earlier this evening I was a simple Boston business man doing business with what I thought to be honorable people. Now I'm reduced to an Indian killer—man killer —because to me an Indian is still a man first and Indian savage second—and I find myself consorting with thieves and murderers, by their own admission." Rogett smiled. "What was that you called yourself? Top gun. And that fancy description of Kantrell's, Kid Kantrell. Both of you sound like children trying to be something you're not."

"You're holding all the cards now, Rogett," Queen said quietly. And Rogett understood that this was no ordinary man full of boasting and talk of bravery. Queen was a cold-blooded killer, dangerous and clever. Rogett wondered how much of the five hundred thousand dollar swindle had been Queen's plan and how much had been Kantrell's.

The limping figure of Skunk moved through the darkness toward the veranda. "You call me, Betajack?"

"I called you, Skunk," Rogett said.

"Oh. How do, Mist' Rogett. Something I can do fer you?"

"You're going to take me to town," Rogett said.

"Town!" Skunk swallowed hard. "But Mist' Rogett—" he turned his appeal to Queen. "Listen, Betajack—"

"Don't talk to me, you old bastard. He's got a gun on me."

"He has!" Skunk turned and tried to see it from his position in the dirt before the steps. "I'll be damned."

"Go inside and take what you'll need for a trip into town, Skunk," Rogett said. "Guns, food or anything else —Queen won't mind, will you?"

Queen was silent. Skunk hesitated. "Tell him to go on, Queen," Rogett urged.

"Get going, you sonofabitch!" Queen said sourly. "You want to get me shot?"

Skunk shuffled up the steps, chuckling to himself, but he didn't answer Queen's question. "I don't think he likes you, Queen," Rogett said.

Skunk returned a few minutes later with two carbines, web belts of cartridges, a canteen of water and loaf of bread. "All I could find. If Meathead catches up with us, we'll put up a fuss with this I reckon."

"Pick out the two best horses," Rogett said.

"Them two on the end."

"Very well." Rogett stopped rocking in the chair and stood. "Anyone that follows me will get shot in the head," Rogett said to Queen.

"You won't get far. Not with Meathead hanging around. And as soon as you hit the trail, he'll know about you."

"At least it will be Meathead and not you," Rogett said.

"Makes no difference to me, so long as we git rid of you," Queen said and turned to Skunk. "Ain't no use coming back, you ratting sonofabitch. If I ever see you again, I'll break you in two."

"Yup, always did know you had a mean temper,

Queen. Never cared much for you neither. But like Mist'
Rogett said, when you come breaking, you better sneak
up on me from behind, because if I see you first, you big
overgrown baboon, I'll take your head off!"

They were on their horses. "You lead the way," Rogett
said. "Anyway, at all. You lead and I'll follow."

"This way, Mist' Rogett," Skunk said. "We'll take to the
fence line across the hills and double back."

"So long," Queen said, almost friendly.

Rogett and Skunk swung their horses around and
beat a heavy tattoo across the packed earth of the door-
yard and disappeared in the shadows.

Chapter Seven

THEY RODE THE FENCE LINE for an hour before Skunk turned sharply away and broke out into the open country that was full of grass and cattle. Rogett followed, riding easily, and then after a few miles, became aware that they were making a big circle and heading back toward the Kantrell ranch. He waited a few minutes to make sure and then rode up alongside Skunk, his hand on his gun. "Hold on, Skunk."

The old man pulled back on his leather. "What's the matter?" the old man inquired.

"We're heading back toward the big house," he said flatly. "You've been making a circle for the last few miles."

"I know it. But I got to meet Miss Tasi."

"Miss Tasi!"

"She came begging a horse just before Queen sent for me. But I couldn't give her one, not with all Queen's riders hanging around and them with orders to keep her on the place."

"So that's where she went."

"I told her to slip out in the dark and shanksmare it to a little creek waller just this side of the house."

"How far is it?"

"We're nearly there."

"All right, but you should have told me."

"I can't tell anyone anything these days," Skunk said. "Every time you tell a man something, it comes back at you."

"I should have listened to you about the Indians—" Rogett said.

"No. You're a man and you got a right to do what you damn please," Skunk said. "I like that in a feller." He glanced at Rogett. "Even if he is a fancy talker."

"I have to warn you, Skunk, Queen and his men may try to come after us—and if we escape them, there are still the Indians."

"Let me worry about Meathead—and Queen," Skunk growled. "Actually I been meaning to git out of there for a long time. I don't like the way things have been going."

"But you told me you liked your job."

"Yeah—but that was before I found out you was a fire eater that would stand up to Queen."

"And what about Miss Tasi?"

"I owe her something too. And when she told me about you—why, I figured it was time to change horses."

"I won't forget—" Rogett started. "I'll be indebted to you—"

"Aw! Shut up. Fancy talk is fine sometime, but after a while it gets on a feller's nerves."

"It's getting light. We'd better hurry," Rogett said.

"No hurry. We can't get out of this grass country until daylight anyway. Have to wait and have light to pick out a trail through the hills. Meathead ain't likely to be up that far, especially in the daylight, especially with his buck son missing. I calculate he don't know that his boy's got himself a place in the happy huntin' grounds—" Skunk laughed—"or he woulda hit that big house long before this."

"We can talk later. Keep moving," Rogett urged.

"I'm moving my animal right smart," Skunk said defensively. "If we got to take a double load with Miss Tasi, and got to climb them hills and keep pushing without any rest, you jest let me decide how fast the trot's going to be and we'll get along just fine."

Rogett grinned, in spite of his anxiety, at the old man's contrary manner and opinions. Probably good opinions, too, Rogett thought.

It was full grey morning, a few minutes before the sun had climbed above the rim of the low hills and the morning-fresh dew was thick and wet. They reached the creek and slipped down into a bed of brush, and while Skunk chased out a stubborn bull, Rogett slipped from the saddle and slapped water onto his face. There was no sign of the girl.

"Where she be, dammit!" Skunk complained. He moved through the edge of the creekbrush and out of sight. Rogett stood beside his horse and waited. The sun burst open on the sky and the brown haze he had thought was some growing vegetation in the grass revealed itself to be an endless herd of cattle. He had never seen so many before in his life. There must have been ten thousand, Rogett considered later, when he remembered the scene.

"She ain't here. But she's been here. I found tracks down the other side of the crik."

"Where could she be?"

"She had to walk it—and she had to be careful. It could be that she just ain't got here yet. Might as well make ourselves comfortable awhile."

"But what about the tracks?"

"Coulda been any one of Bet's hands." Skunk shook his shoulder with annoyance. "Tracks didn't look none too fresh anyway."

"Skunk—listen to me a minute. There's something crazy going on here."

"Say that again, Mist' Rogett."

"No, listen to me, this is serious."

Skunk splashed water onto his face. "I'm listening."

"Last night, Tasi came to my room."

"I know it. She told me. I told you she set me right about you."

"Kantrell came in, just as she was explaining how Kantrell and Queen planned to swindle me out of the money I paid as option rights to mine the hills."

"I'll be damned!" Skunk said, all attention. His crafty old eyes set on Rogett. "Go ahead."

"Kantrell thought Tasi and I were having a secret rendezvous and threatened me—"

"Secret what?"

"Never mind. He thought Tasi and I were—well—about to go to bed together."

Skunk grunted.

"Tasi left—then Kantrell left after her. I waited ten minutes, planning to come out to the stable and have you prepare horses for Tasi and myself—but I stopped by her door and went in. The room was dark—and someone hit me on the head and knocked me out."

Skunk pursed his dry lips.

"When I came out of it—not more than a few minutes later, I heard someone in the hall. It was Queen, going to my room, his gun in his hand, looking for me. When he came back by the door, I braced him." Rogett paused. "You know the rest."

Skunk nodded. "Who you think it was that hit you?"

"I thought you might be able to tell me that."

Skunk was suddenly alert. He looked as if he had stopped breathing—and then pointed on the other side of the creek bed. "Something over there," he whispered.

"Perhaps it's Tasi."

"No—wrong direction." Skunk said.

"Well—what?"

"Ain't none of Bet's hands out here—so it can only mean one thing—" The old man moved faster than Rogett had seen him move before and pull up into the saddle. "We'd better git the hell out of here fast. Git mounted, man, we got to move—"

There was no mistaking the fear—no, Rogett thought, *terror* in the old man's voice. Skunk jerked the horse around savagely and started away from the hills. Rogett leaped into the saddle and raced after the old man.

It did not take long for Rogett to see that Skunk was headed toward Kantrell's ranch. He lashed his pony hard and urged it ahead. It took hard riding, but he drew up alongside the old man's horse and grabbed the bridle. "Whoa up!" he bellowed.

Skunk tried to lash him with the end of his leather reins. Rogett held on tight. Skunk lashed out again. The old man spurred the horse hard, and it was the force of the lunge of the animal that broke Rogett's grip. But Skunk's flailing arm passed Rogett and he grabbed, hard, yanking the old man from the saddle. They both went down in a heap. The horses trotted away a few steps and stood still.

Rogett grabbed Skunk by the shirt and shook him until the old man stopped resisting. "Let go of me—you damn fool—I know what I'm doing—"

"Why did you try and run out on me?" Rogett demanded.

"Let me go!" Skunk jerked wildly against Rogett's grip.

Rogett slapped the old man hard across the face. Skunk looked at him, shock on his face. Slowly, Rogett saw the terror fade from his eyes. *Now tell me!*

"Look—there's your answer!" Skunk pointed back toward the creek.

Rogett turned to look. Skunk jerked away, ran hard for his horse and leaped into the saddle. He drew the carbine and threw a shell into the chamber, leveled it at Rogett. "Ain't you wondered why Queen and his hands didn't come after us? If what you say is true, about them trying to swindle you, how could they let you get away? So why didn't they come fagging their horses after us, eh? Them tough waddies and all their guns, eh?"

Rogett made a move for his horse. Skunk slapped the animal on the rump and watched it move a hundred feet away and come to a standstill. "They didn't come after us because they knew probably after their ride last night that Meathead and his braves were all over the place—out here in the grass—as well as along the trail to town. I seen signs back there—but they coulda been old signs. But then I saw something move. I'm heading back for the ranch, Mist' Rogett. Sorry I couldn't help you—"

"But what—about Tasi?"

"She'll be all right—Meathead won't hurt her—"

Skunk spun the pony around, threw the canteen of water to the ground along with the loaf of bread and some spare shells. "If you want to get to town, there's three ways. One, back through the ranch and Kantrell and Queen waiting for you. Two, through the grass where Meathead is waiting. The third way is straight up through them hills yonder where there ain't no water—no food—and nobody but the Indians know how to get into and out of!"

Skunk spun the pony around, slapped it hard with the leather and disappeared a few minutes later in the belly-deep buffalo grass.

Rogett, stupefied, watched the old man ride away. He was alone. The brown haze had turned into a solid line against the gently swaying green grass of the valley. He turned and stared up at the hills.

He walked toward the pony, speaking to it gently so that it would not be frightened, reached the leather and swung into the saddle. He hesitated. Three ways to go, each of them leading to Jicarilla. One went through the grass to a sure ambush by Meathead. The second back to the Kantrell ranch and Queen. He turned the pony toward the hills. "The first two are real dangers, horse," he said softly, studying the low rise and the gradual hump of the mounds that disappeared into the depths of the greater range of mountains further on. "The third is a lot of the same real dangers—with the added risk of dying of thirst or getting lost."

He stopped the pony dead in its tracks. A strange nervousness gripped him. He thought about the cowardice of Skunk and his muscles tightened.

Once he almost turned the horse back toward the ranch. Twice he thought about trying it through the grass and risking an ambush—he had a full day's light ahead of him.

But finally he made a decision. He turned toward the hills.

He rode steadily, glancing back over his shoulder now and then, wary of his trail, pushing through the herds of cattle that moved away from him like a tide of water rippling back from the bow of a down-East fishing boat.

The sun was high before he closed on the hills and entered the dead, unmoving quiet of the tight trails and small box canyons.

Chapter Eight

HE HAD RIDDEN for an hour. He saw nothing, heard nothing. No sound, no movement. Not even the brush of wings from a high eagle's nest, or the rustle of a little animal running into the brush. No stray cattle, no wandering dogies. Anonymous, thumping silence that could have been the indication of a funeral rite in another world. The rocks were bald, hard, flinty. There was very little loose gravel. The trail, if it could be called a trail, was deep in pure red sand, sometimes mixed with yellow, and sometimes pure white. Nowhere did he see so much as a footprint of an animal, or even the marks of a snake. The sand was always smooth, always wind-blown. There was no shade. No growth of vegetation of any kind. It was the most barren place Rogett had ever seen. Never once did he stop moving his head and eyes, searching every dark hole on a lofty rock above the way he wanted to pass. He climbed steadily, and watched the sun carefully for his direction, which was due north and therefore easy to follow.

He had been traveling well and had grown used to silence, which had begun to comfort him rather than arouse his fears. As long as it remains silent, Rogett thought, nothing can happen. He even begun whistling, but soon abandoned this. Somehow it did not fit with the unbroken, ebony-like surface of the silence. There was evidence of gold. Several times he had wanted to stop and examine a piece of rock. It was certainly one of the richest-looking prospects he had seen in years. And then, bitterly reflecting on the attitude and the underhanded intentions of Kantrell, he forgot for a few minutes to notice the trail, in relation to the sun, and when he looked up suddenly, coming out of his reflections, he saw that he was in a small box canyon about a thousand yards deep and several hundred yards wide with no passage through. He turned the animal slowly in the narrow confines of the trail and started to backtrack. But he couldn't find his tracks. The sand had blown over the marks and completely covered his trail.

He ignored the sand and stared at the rock. He had cut off from a broad ten-yard-wide break through the hills about the time he began to think about Kantrell. He was a man used to rock and stone and could, in a sense, read it like a book, but after an hour's backtracking, he could find no place that he was sure he had passed before.

He stopped and studied the sun. It was high, directly overhead, and a glance at his watch told him it was near enough to noon for it to be impossible to read the sun's traverse for another hour until its descent became more pronounced. He slipped from the saddle, examined his immediate surroundings and opened the canteen of water. He used his cupped hands to give the horse a drink, spilling a great deal of it to the sand, and then drank sparingly himself. He decided he would wait before eating the bread. If he was lucky, he might make Jicarilla before night, and he knew the bread would make him thirsty.

And now, with even the slow thump of the horse's hooves removed, the deadening, numbing silence bore down on him.

He began to think about his condition. Doubt began to enter into his thoughts as to whether he should have braved Meathead's Apaches, or gone back to face Queen. After all, this wasn't his country. And if an old timer like Skunk had been frightened off, what right had he to wander into the hills alone? He had confidence in his ability to handle guns; Queen's Colt, a carbine and a plentiful supply of shells, in addition to the Derringer, comforted him in that way, and the horse was a fine animal. But—

The movement was so slight that he was sure he had imagined it. But when he thought about it, he was sure that he hadn't.

He stood. He pulled the heavy Colt and looked around. He was in a little clearing that was covered with fine white sand. To his back was a sheer height of solid rock that looked several hundred feet high. Before him, opposite the wall, a series of huge boulders in steps that rose to even greater heights, forming a curious kind of triangle. In the clearing, he stood at the base of only one side. The way that he had just come, circling through smaller rocks, and the only way out of the clearing, dropping down, he could see was more of the same.

Rogett stood perfectly still for five minutes, his back to the straight wall, watching the step-like effect of the boulders, and glancing to his right and left at the trail. He saw nothing. Nothing moved.

"Let's go, horse," he said aloud, more to reassure himself that he could still speak than from any thought of taking courage from his own voice. But the sound of his voice was so startling, so cold, as if it had been the voice of a stranger, that it was all he could do to keep from leaping into the saddle and riding furiously down the trail.

But the tight discipline he had learned over his emotions and feelings in Boston came to the fore and he forced himself to move slowly, deliberately, so that haste would not precipitate some irreconcilable damage. He mounted slowly, clucked his tongue, dry though he had just had a drink of water, and moved the animal away from the side of the rock face. The sun bore down on him relentlessly.

Then he saw the movement again. He drew Betajack's gun and fired before he realized he had put his finger on the trigger.

The shot exploded, echoing and re-echoing over and over in the hills like rolls of summer thunder. The noise of the shot and the unexpected hair-trigger on Betajack's gun caused Rogett to stand, half stunned, motionless until the last echo had died.

Then he remembered that he had seen a movement beyond a ledge of rock twenty yards ahead of him.

He jerked the gun up again, took a deep breath and forced himself to speak. He hoped his voice would be firm. "All right, who ever you are—whatever you are, come out, or I'll fire again and I assure you I won't miss."

He waited. Nothing moved. He strained his eyes in the harsh brightness of the sun. "This is the last warning," Rogett managed to say and was not at all sure that there was any authority in his voice.

He took dead aim on the edge of the rock where he had seen the movement and fired. Stone splintered and dusted away from the edge.

Again he waited—and then heard a scratching noise as if someone was working their way across stone. Rogett took a deep breath, threw a glance over his shoulders, both right and left, to make sure he was not covered from the rear, then nudged the horse forward.

Tasi Kantrell stepped out from behind the rock, her hands high over her head. She was not smiling. She saw at once that Rogett had Betajack's gun. Her eyes opened wide. Slowly she lowered her arms. "You!" she said, alarm in her voice.

Rogett stared at her stupidly. "Are you hurt?"

Her alarm forgotten, Tasi walked toward his horse and grabbed the animal's harness. "Where is Skunk? Didn't he come with you?" she asked.

"He went back," Rogett said.

"Back where?"

"To the ranch."

She frowned. "Why would he do a thing like that?"

Rogett looked around at the dead hills. He tried to keep his voice under control, but he was not sure of it.

61

There was a bit of emotion in his voice when he spoke and he hoped Tasi did not notice it. "He was afraid of Meathead."

"Did you see any signs?"

"He saw something move down in the creek—he thought it would be Meathead and his braves—out in the grass. Tasi—" Rogett said suddenly, "is it—do we have any kind of a chance in these hills?"

He didn't know what made him blurt out such a question to the girl, and once he had said it, he wondered what her reaction would be. He was even more confused when she frowned and spoke thoughtfully. "Well, I've been coming up here for years. Since I was a little girl. Nothing's happened to me."

"But your father!"

"If you mean Kantrell, he's not my father," she said sharply.

"All right then. Mister Kantrell: the point is, he doesn't want you to come up here. Why?"

"You'll have to ask him that," Tasi replied.

"I hope sincerely that I will never have the opportunity."

"Meaning just what, Mister Rogett?"

"Meaning that if there is any way possible for me to get into town other than returning to the ranch, I intend using it. But back to my question. Why would Kantrell want to keep you from coming into the hills?"

Tasi's voice was bitter. "He's afraid I'll find the treasure of Aahasi and leave him."

"You believe there *is* a treasure?" Rogett asked. "That it actually exists?"

She looked at him sharply. "You found gold here, didn't you? Enough to bring you all the way out from the East and invest a half million dollars?"

Rogett nodded, reluctantly.

"If there's gold here," Tasi went on, "evidence of it to suit you, then why wouldn't there be a treasure? One that my father, Aahasi, knew about?"

"Yes, why not," Rogett heard himself saying. The girl made sense. Tasi rounded his horse and unslung the canteen of water. She took a deep drink. Rogett watched her. "But what are you going to do now?" he asked when she had finished.

"I don't know."

"Would you return to the ranch?"

She smiled ironically. "I always have in the past. There is no place else I can go."

"Certainly you could go into town."

"And do what? He'd only send Betajack and a few of his hands in after me. And if anyone helped me out—like giving me something to eat or a place to stay—he would see to it that it never happened again and whoever helped me would regret it."

"Well, you certainly can't remain in these Godforsaken hills," Rogett said firmly. "Do you know how to get into town without returning to the ranch?"

"Through the grass."

"Skunk thought enough of the possibility for an ambush that he returned to the ranch rather than try the grass," Rogett said. "How about through these hills? Skunk said there was a way. Do you think you could find it?"

"I think so," Tasi said.

"We would have to be careful of any of Meathead's band of savages," Rogett warned.

"Don't worry about Meathead," Tasi replied.

"I will, just the same, if you don't mind," Rogett replied.

Suddenly Tasi smiled. Rogett found himself grinning back at her sudden warmth. And once more, as he had been the first time he saw her, he was struck with her beauty. "Come on." He held out his hand. "Up you come!" He lifted her to the back of the horse. When she had settled, he asked, "Which way?"

"Straight ahead until you come to a queer-looking rock that sort of looks like an Indian's face."

After they had ridden a few minutes and picked up the landmark, Tasi slipped from the horse and climbed to a high point for a look around the hills for any sign of Meathead before they went on. Something then occurred to Rogett that he had forgotten to ask her. She walked back in the sand and Rogett pointed to her footprints. "What about them?" he said, pointing toward her footprints. "Aren't you afraid of being followed?"

She laughed, pointed. Rogett could see that already the wind was washing away her footprints. "They'll be gone in no time."

"Now which way?" Rogett asked when she had swung back behind him.

"Straight ahead, I think." Tasi said cautiously. "Just follow the trail and keep bearing to the right. We've got to cross over the hump somewhere along the line."

"The hump?"

"The top of the hills. You've got to go up before you can come down. And town is on the other side of the hills."

"Do you think the horse will take both of us for any length of time? You know your ranch animals well enough to make a decision about that. Is this animal a good one?"

Tasi patted the horse on the rump. "This mount will take two more like us and keep plugging, Mister Rogett."

"Very well, now keep a sharp eye out for signs of Meathead."

Tasi chuckled. "I didn't mean to say we have to completely ignore Meathead, Mister Rogett," the girl said, "but it isn't likely we'll have any trouble with him. They don't come up here often." She looked around the hills. "And I've never seen too many of Meathead's Apaches this far up into the hills. They spook mighty easy—except when they're mad."

"From what Skunk had to say about the situation, the lot of them might be on the warpath for my having killed old Meathead's son. So if that is the case, we can expect to see them up here."

Tasi shook her head. "That's something else again." And Rogett felt her arms tighten around his waist.

Chapter Nine

THEY RODE IN SILENCE for nearly two hours, climbing steadily. Each time it seemed to Rogett that they had reached a peak, his hope that it would be the last one was replaced by another rise still higher in the distance that they would have to scale.

Tasi spoke only when it was time to change their direction along the trail and in the climb. Several times she seemed to become confused and slipped off the horse and climbed to a high point to study the surrounding country, checking for landmarks. She would then return to Rogett who waited patiently, give their direction and they would move out.

It was unmercifully hot. They were forced to stop frequently to give the horse a rest and it was during one of these stops, while they were sitting in the shade of an overhanging rock ledge and had finished their cautious sipping of the water from the canteen, that Tasi began to talk.

She talked easily, with Rogett plying her with gentle questioning. She used expressions that his Eastern ear was unaccustomed to and these she had to explain. They sat, waiting for the horse to ease off its heavy blowing. Waiting for the heat to begin to lift from the afternoon.

"Kantrell has always wanted me to call him father. But when I grew old enough to hear—and to understand the stories about my mother and father—real father, Aahasi, I stopped. He changed after that."

"How old were you when you realized he was not your

father?" Rogett asked her.

"About twelve. I remember I used to like to come up into the hills. I didn't know why." Tasi took a deep breath. "I would sneak down to the corral and take a horse, sometimes even bareback, and walk him out into the grass and far enough away from the house to keep from being overheard and come up here and just wander around."

"How did you hear about the question of Jezebel?"

"It was in Jicarilla. Kantrell used to go in every Saturday for supplies and of course I would go in with him. I used to go play with some children while Kantrell did his buying. We were playing Indians one afternoon and choosing up sides the way kids will do and one little girl wanted to play Jezebel. I didn't know who Jezebel was—the only one I knew about was in the Bible—and I couldn't see the connection between playing Indian and her wanting to play Jezebel." Tasi drew in a deep breath. Her voice hardened a little. "So they told me. And how they told me. They all knew it of course, having heard it from their own folks. And it was pretty common gossip around town. They used all the four letter words and ugly descriptions that children will use when they've turned—and for no reason—on another. Cruel, heartless. I got the whole story in about ten minutes. They didn't miss a detail. I've learned later that they didn't."

"Of course you went to Kantrell and asked him about it," Rogett asked.

"Right away. I found him in the dry goods store buying pants. The store was full of men. I'll never forget the scene as long as I live. They were laughing and talking —the way men do when they get together—and when I came in, they stopped. Kantrell turned to me and smiled and asked me if I wanted a peppermint stick. I remember saying no, I didn't want a peppermint, I just wanted to know who my father was."

Rogett remained silent. Tasi was deep in thought. It was a moment before she continued. "Well, there was a slight pause and you could have heard a pin drop. Then they started laughing. Not at me, but at Kantrell. Then I started crying. I got hysterical. I don't know why. I've often thought back over that moment and wondered. I think it was because they were laughing at him. I still considered him my father at that time. And—" She stoppped.

Rogett leaned over and touched her arm. "You don't have to tell me any more," he said.

She shook her head. "Oh, it's nothing. It's just that all my life, it seems, I've had this damn mystery hanging over my head. Every girl I knew in school in Jicarilla has been married a long time now. Some of them have two and three babies."

"I can imagine how difficult it must have been for you after that experience," Rogett said.

"No, you can't," Tasi said sharply. "A human being can never know what another human being suffers. I used to look at the kids that had fathers that were town drunks. They didn't have shoes to wear, or pants, or anything to eat. But they were accepted. People loved them—well—just because they were kids. The town stopped loving me —if it ever did. I became the daughter of Jezebel. But I stuck it out," Tasi said doggedly. "I went to school, and when there was a party, I went to the party, or picnic or whatever it was, and though half the time I didn't say one word to anyone, I'd stay. I'd force them to be uncomfortable. You know," she turned and appealed to Rogett, "by not letting them forget about me."

They were silent a while and then moved to the horse, slipped into the saddle and began moving on up the side of the hill. It was some time before Tasi began talking again. She sat close to Rogett, leaning her bare cheek on his shoulder and talking softly, so softly that Rogett had the feeling that she was talking to herself. But she would stop and ask him, "You know what I mean?" And he would say that he understood.

"There was a hell of a hard time when school was over and t re wasn't any way that I could force myself on them any more," Tasi said, with the first trace of bitterness in her voice that Rogett had heard. "A lot of the boys and girls started pairing off, and got married, and then everyone would get together again for the wedding, or the quilting bee for the newlyweds, or a shower for the brides. The same bunch, you know what I mean, Mister Rogett? Only I was never invited."

Rogett thought back to his own youth. It had been the complete opposite. He was the first one invited on any list of invitations, and he remembered with a tinge of guilt that there had been several in his circle, even as a child, that had been excluded. He could not recall now, try as he might, why this one or that one had been rejected by the group. He had never thought of them until that moment. And he wondered about the men and the women—if they ever had the same feelings as Tasi was now telling him about. He was sure they did.

And suddenly Sidney Rogett felt guilty.

"There were a few boys that came around. And I have to say that Kantrell went out of his way to be nice to them. But it always turned out to be the same thing. They weren't interested in me, they only wanted to get at Kantrell's money and the ranch. Kantrell didn't seem to mind when he found out about it, but I chased them all away."

Rogett patted her hand. "Good girl," he said.

"Then Betajack came along."

"Did he make a proposal of marriage to you?"

"Every day at dinner and twice on Sundays," Tasi said.

Rogett grunted. It was an angry grunt. His thoughts of Betajack were dark. He tightened up even then on thinking of the naked menace the man had shown the night before. "Did you like him?"

"I wouldn't look at him cross-eyed," Tasi said bitterly.

They rode further in silence. The sun was just beginning to drop a little and the heat was suffocating. They stopped for a short rest and found shade easily now that the sun was behind some of the highest peaks. They had climbed a great distance, and when Rogett turned back to look, he could see the heat rising from what he knew to be the flats and the grass country where the giant herd grazed—and beyond this—the Kantrell ranch.

She talked about life on the ranch and how much she loved it—and hoped to settle with a good man. "But that seems far away, everything considered, Mister Rogett. Everybody around here knows the story of Jezebel. If I ever do have a good life—one of peace—I'll have to leave these hills, and the grass country and all my friends to find it."

Rogett reached out and touched her hand. "You're a brave woman, Tasi. I shall always consider it an honor to have known you."

She talked on. The two of them sat in the shade, fighting against the heat, drowsy, their voices soft.

Tasi paused in her conversation. The sun had dropped fast. The heat was easing off. She looked around suddenly as if making sure of her bearings, and then suggested they hurry along.

The horse continued down a small boxed-in trail, moving easily. They did not talk any more. Tasi was intent on searching for signs and often turned on the back of the horse to look around the area. She would nod to herself and then indicate that Rogett should go on.

"The toughest part—" Tasi said. She took a deep breath. "The mother part of it I didn't mind so much—it bothered me as a child. Everyone else had a mother—all I had was a mystery. But the day came—as I had always hoped it would come—when I didn't have to be concerned about having—or not having—a mother. And when it came, something else came—a new kind of terror—to take its place."

"What was that?" Rogett asked as gently as he could.

"Bet Jack Queen."

"In what way?"

"The insistence—no," Tasi hesitated, "I can't say there was any insistence from Kantrell for me to marry Bet. It was a lack of it. Anything Bet wanted to do—or say to me—was all right, Kantrell never said anything. And one

70

day when I did mention it to Kantrell, went right up to him and asked him to keep Bet away from me, or at least keep him from bothering me, Kantrell just dismissed it. 'Bet's all right,' he said."

Rogett did not make a comment. He could well imagine how a man like Bet Jack Queen would behave around a woman—especially one as beautiful as Tasi and as rich.

"Once when we had a party at the ranch—it was one of the few times that Kantrell allowed me to have one—there was a cow waddy that came from another ranch and that was trying to spark me. I liked him all right. He was a nice enough man—and very kind and gentle—" Tasi paused. "I often think back to that night. I'm sure that Clem loved me."

"Was that his name? Clem?"

"Yes. Clem Runch. Texan. Anyway, he danced with me once too often that night at the party and Bet took him out in back of the barn, picked a fight with him and beat him nearly half to death. It was a warning, Bet said, for everyone that had ideas about me. That was when I went to Kantrell and he said Bet was all right. That night I took a gun and went looking for Bet but he took it away from me before I could use it. They thought that was very funny, defending my honor that way. I wasn't defending my honor. I wanted to kill him for beating up Clem so bad he was sick half a year and finally left this part of the country altogether. I saw him once more after that. I tried to talk to him—on the street in town—but he turned and ran from me. He yelled for me to stay away from him—he didn't want to die for some whim of a woman—"

Rogett shook his head. This was certainly a violent and wild country.

"You can imagine what the town had to say about that!" Tasi said bitterly. "From then on there was no stopping Bet. He would grab for me every chance he caught me alone. He would never do anything before Kantrell—but boy, you just let him catch me out alone somewhere—I've come home with bruises on my arms

71

and shoulders more than once. And he's come back scratched like he had a fight with a tom cat."

Rogett felt the anger rise in his throat. "Wasn't there anyone you could turn to?"

"Who would stand up to Bet's gun? The fastest gun in this part of the country—and the meanest with his fists. No, Mister Rogett, there wasn't anyone I could turn to. I'm a staked woman. And if something terrible doesn't happen to Bet—or to myself—I might end up with him just to keep from being an old maid."

They rode on in silence and finally Rogett could not hold back any more. He turned. "Look here, Tasi, how much further do we have to go?"

Tasi jerked upright and looked around. Rogett did not have to be told that the girl had no idea where she was. He knew from her expression that she was quite lost.

It seemed that the sun was working against them now. They had to backtrack—and fast—with Tasi searching for a familiar landmark or trail sign. They moved fast to beat the rapidly fading light, but Rogett knew from Tasi's wild searching that she had no idea which way to go and that one way was as good as another. It was hopeless to continue searching for a trail or some sign that she would recognize. It was beginning to get cold. The sudden drop of the sun had left them not only in near darkness, but without means of protection against the night. Tasi wore only the light blouse and buckskin riding skirt and Rogett could see her beginning to shiver in the evening chill.

He stripped off his jacket and handed it up to her. "Put this on," he said. "We're stopping now before we're in complete darkness. Quick now, take care of the horse while I look for firewood."

Tasi, Rogett saw, for the first time, showed signs of being afraid. "I'm sorry," she said. "I thought I knew the hills."

"Don't worry about that now."

Rogett turned and began to backtrack over their trail

and search for anything that would burn. He searched for an hour and by then it was completely dark and he had found nothing. When he returned, Tasi was huddled beneath a horse blanket, her back to a rock wall.

"This way," Tasi said, hearing his teeth chattering from twenty feet away.

Rogett found her in the darkness and flopped to the sand. He pulled the blanket over his shoulders. Neither of them had eaten for twenty-four hours, and as hungry as Rogett was, he was determined not to say anything until Tasi spoke up. Even then there was little he could personally do about it. He had been in the hills nearly a full day and hadn't seen a living thing. He remembered the loaf of bread Skunk had taken from the Kantrell ranch along with the two carbines and canteen of water. Luckily the old man had slung the canteen over Rogett's pony and kept the bread with him. Without water, the day—and this moment—would have been murder for both of them.

Little by little the chill wore off and his teeth stopped chattering.

"I think," Tasi said quietly, "that if we got closer together, we might be warmer. "And then she took his arm and pulled it around her shoulder, snuggled closer and pressed her body up against Rogett. They lay still for what seemed like a minute and then he awoke with a start. The wind was up and he was cold. Tasi slept in his arms.

His arm ached and was numb from holding the weight of her body as the girl relaxed; he tried to ease himself into another position, found that he couldn't, then slipped away from her altogether, put her head on the sand and covered her with the blanket.

He looked at his watch. In the bright starlight he could just manage to see the hands.

Ten-thirty. My God! he thought. More than eight hours before the sun comes up again.

He began to pace up and down, slapping his arms back and forth to keep the circulation going.

73

"Sidney," Tasi said softly from the darkness. "Sidney. Don't be foolish. Come here with me. You'll freeze to death."

"I'm perfectly all right, Tasi. I want to think. There is much that I have to think about."

"You won't be able to think if you try to keep awake all night and fight off this night air. Come here."

He stumbled to her side. He felt her hands on his, pulling him down to his knees beside her. "Here," she said softly, sleepily. She held the blanket up for him. "Come down beside me."

He slipped into the warmth of the blanket and felt her arms encircle him, felt the warmth of her body close to his. In a moment his teeth stopped chattering for the second time and he relaxed.

In the darkness, beyond his vision and his thoughts, Tasi smiled a little smile as she held him close to her. Gradually his body stopped shivering and she knew he was asleep.

Chapter Ten

ROGETT'S SLEEP WAS FAR from being undisturbed and he awoke often. But he did not move. Once, having no idea what time it was, he tried speaking to her, but there was no reply to his softly spoken, "Tasi?"

He remained still, warmed by the thick blanket and her body pressing close to his back, hungry, but not too uncomfortable, and thought of the difference between this girl and Antonia.

He thought too of what would be said of him if they knew, Antonia and those whom he called his friends back in the East, that he had spent a night in a deserted, haunting, isolated hill country, sleeping with a girl beneath a horse blanket. He remembered laughing at the idea of the New England tradition of bundling. But then there had been a board between the parties sharing the bed.

The embrace of her arms around his shoulders, the press of her body against his made him sharply aware that there was no board between him and Tasi.

She moved, stirring in her sleep. Then a moment later as he lay perfectly still so as not to awaken her: "Sidney?"

"Yes."

"Are you all right?"

"Yes. Are you?"

"I've been dreaming."

"I hope it was pleasant."

"I was a little girl again. I was out with the cowhands in the bunkhouse and they were showing me how to handle a rope. Then cookie rang the dinner bell and they all left me alone. I kept trying to twirl the rope—and then my mother came out of the house and took me into the kitchen and washed my face and hands."

"Your mother?"

"Yes. I don't remember her too well. But I remember her."

She was silent and he thought she had gone back to sleep again. Then she spoke. "I feel sometimes as—as if I belonged in the hills."

"Is that why you keep coming back?"

She didn't answer. He waited for what seemed like an eternity and then realized she was asleep again. He rested his head on his arm and closed his eyes. But sleep would not come. He kept seeing a string of lights—now winking at him—now disappearing.

He opened his eyes. He still saw the lights.

He then realized that he had been watching them for some time without knowing it. "Tasi!" he said quietly, urgently. "Tasi!"

She stirred. "What is it—where—?"

He put his hand over her mouth. "Look!" he whispered, bending close to her ear. "Lights!"

She raised up slowly and stared. In the distance the lights grew brighter and seemed to be approaching them. The wind had died down and there was no sound in the hills.

"What is it?" he asked.

"I don't know. It looks like a file of men carrying torches."

"Yes—yes." Rogett heard himself say in a voice that was strange and unlike his own. "Who are they?"

"I don't know."

"Are they coming this way?"

"I can't tell." Tasi was standing now. She moved in the darkness, her hand gripping his tightly. Together they inched their way forward to a rock and climbed it.

"My God!" Rogett said. "There must be a hundred of them!"

76

Tasi said nothing. She watched the moving lights, bobbing up and down as they would if carried by men cautious in their steps.

"How far away do you think they are?" Rogett asked. He had absolutely no concept of distance in the pitch black night.

"It seems like they're on the other side of that canyon we were boxed into just before we backtracked."

"Yes, I remember it. It seemed to me to be pretty large. At least a half mile across."

They didn't talk any more. They stood transfixed on the rock and watched the procession of lights move through the darkness without apparent ground underneath them, bobbing and weaving, and then slowly, one by one, the lights went out.

"They must have turned a bend in the trail," Tasi suggested.

The experience shook Rogett badly. But he tried to keep it from Tasi. The stupidity of the situation he had gotten himself into with Kantrell struck him again—riding off into the night and shooting two Indians, then returning to the ranch and hearing the story of Jezebel, Kantrell and Aahasi, then a wild escape from the ranch and Kantrell with Bet Jack Queen hot after them. Then the strange behavior of Skunk at the water hole—running back, frightened, a terror-stricken old man that had seen something move near the water, whereas before he had coolly accepted an Indian raid as if it were part of the daily routine. Then the mad scramble into the hills alone, only to discover the strange girl, Tasi, who was a weird combination of childhood bitterness and fiery stubbornness against Kantrell.

It will all work out, he said to himself. It will resolve itself into something that can be explained and easily settled.

But even as he thought about it, he knew that he was whistling in the dark. He was not back in Boston now, where such things could be explained. He was in another world, in another time, and even the people were unlike

77

any people he had ever known before.

They were back at the blanket, but he could not get himself back into the mood of relaxation he had enjoyed before. He pulled out his watch and tried to see its face, but the stars had all vanished from the sky and he could see nothing. The darkness was intense. He could hardly see his hand before his face.

He pulled the carbine out, checked it, and sat cross-legged, determined to wait for dawn.

Tasi said nothing. She went back under the blanket and in a moment, he could hear the deep relaxed breathing of the girl's sleep.

And then Tasi was at his side. "Sidney—wake up!"

He opened his eyes. He had slumped down on the sand and the sun was now up full over the eastern rim of the hills. Tasi was shaking him, excitedly, her face eager and full of impatience—happy, eager impatience.

"What is it?" he jumped up and brought the carbine around.

"Look!" Tasi pointed.

The sun was fully up and over the edge of the last hill by then and Tasi was pointing across the lip of the canyon in the direction of the lights they had seen the night before.

He could see nothing unusual. Bright sun. Deep shadows on the canyon floor. Silence. Stillness that reminded him of a description of an ancient tomb.

"I don't see anything," Rogett said.

"There—at the side of the hill. Up above the black spot that looks like it might be a cave or something."

Her voice was excited. She kept pointing in the same direction and describing the same black spot for him to look at. All Rogett could see was a reflection of the sun—

A reflection of the sun!

He looked again, shielding his eyes. It was as if a second sun was rising with the true one, rising up the side of the hill face, a sheer height of wall that was lost above them hundreds of feet away.

"The legend!" Tasi exclaimed. "The legend! Remember?"

"What legend?" he asked.

The treasure of Aahasi lingers yet for the one that will dig in the shadows before the sun rises!

She did not explain any further, but rushed on. "Look, the reflection off that wall, see, it's so strong that it casts its own shadows back down into the canyon floor. Look! There are two shadows. The one the sun makes—and the one the reflection is making. I've been watching it. It shone in my eyes and woke me up. I thought it was the sun at first, but then I realized the sun was rising in *back* of me. I saw the shadows on the canyon floor before the sun rose above the rim of the hills. The whole floor of the canyon was lighted up as if the sun was already up—!"

Her voice was high pitched. "We've found it, Sidney! We—you and I have found it!"

Rogett was still trying to study the formation of the double shadows on the canyon floor—and attempting to figure it out. Sure enough, there were two shadows on the floor. But it would not last long. Even as he watched, the true sun was rising above the point where it would reflect strongly enough to cause the shadows. He turned to Tasi, whose face was tense with excitement. "Found—found what, Tasi?" he asked, taking her by the arms.

"The treasure of Aahasi—the treasure of my father!"

She turned and ran down the trail and headed for the canyon floor.

Chapter Eleven

THE REFLECTION CAME, as Rogett suspected that it might, from iron pyrites, fool's gold. A thick, wide face of it that looked as if it might be the greatest treasure in the world, but was worthless.

But there was no fear that the iron pyrites was at the end of the legend of Aahasi. They found the entrance to the cave in one of the deep shadows nearby and entered.

Even from the outside they could see that the cave had been used, but not since long ago. There was evidence of an open fire pit, with the base rocks badly scorched and bones nearby as further indication that there had been an attempt to sustain life in an orderly, routine manner. Neither of them wanted to enter the ten- by twelve-foot open face of the cave. There was something, and they both felt this without mentioning it to the other, as grave and as deeply forbidding as cracking the seal on an ancient tomb.

It was dark. A bat flew out from within, then flew back in again, then out again, and then upon trying to regain the entrance to the cave, flew into the side wall and fell brokenly to the ground.

Tasi shuddered, reached out for Rogett's hand and turned away in pale revulsion at the writhing of the bat. Rogett stepped over and brought his heel down hard on the furry creature and killed it.

"Do you want to go on?" he asked. Her hands were cold in his own. "Perhaps I had better go first."

"No—no—I must go," Tasi said in a strange voice. "I

know this is the place—"

"What place, Tasi?"

Their voices had risen and now there came back to them a hollow echo. "Tasi, what place do you mean?"

Her face was ashen color. Her eyes were wide with fear—or was it something else? Rogett did not hesitate. He spun her around and slapped her across the face.

The sound of the slap echoed and re-echoed in the hollow cave and then came back to them, even to the sudden and gasping cry Tasi gave a split second after he had struck her.

"Oh!"

And then *Oh!* again—then again, *Oh!* only fainter, and then the sound died and they were left alone again with the stunning silence of the cave, the canyon and the forbidding hills.

Tasi took another step forward, alone. She glanced down. An earthen jar, broken, and once perhaps used for water, skittered across the hard surface of the cave floor where she had touched it with her boot. Their eyes had become used to the light now and they could see some distance into the interior of the cave. They saw more evidence of habitation. There were several hunting bows, the draw strings on them long ago rotted and broken by the pull of the bows' curve. A pistol lay in the middle of the cave floor, rusted, its hammer still jacked back, as if someone had tried to use it and couldn't and had dropped it.

There was a huge water pot to one side, standing beneath a worn surface which Rogett could easily see had been made by the trickling of water from above. The occupants had had the ultimate luxury of running water dripping eternally into the huge pot, but the source had dried up years ago. There was a scurrying around in the bottom of the huge bowl and Rogett quickly picked up a heavy lid and clamped it over the top with a cloud of dust flowing up around him.

He shuddered and was not at all curious as to what was inside.

Tasi had moved on ahead of him, moving from one object in the cool cave to another, examining a kitchen tool, a simple mechanism for re-leading spent shells and the lead mold for shaping the slugs, an empty gunpowder cask, a gourd for dipping water, now cracked along the bowl.

Rogett stooped to pick up the pistol, wiping away the dust. He eased the hammer down, but it would not close completely and he had to force it down. The shells inside the chamber were probably so old they would not fire anyway.

"Sidney!" Tasi's voice was short with alarm.

He stumbled forward. She was standing just beyond a slightly jutting wall of the cave that partitioned the area into two room-like sections. She pointed. Rogett stepped to her side and gripped her around the shoulders.

Upon, what must have been a bed of furs, were two skeletons. One was much larger than the other and dressed in the rotting strings of what must have been buckskin breeches and blouse.

The smaller skeleton was still shrouded within a good portion of what must have been a buckskin, sack-like dress. There were beads and—some of the strings had rotted away, but there were still a few clinging to the old skin fiber—every indication that a man and a woman had been slain on the bed.

Even in the semi-light, Rogett could see the two holes in the back of each skull.

Tasi was unmoved. Then she began to tremble. She twisted free of Rogett's arms and moved toward the skeletal remains. Rogett grabbed her and pulled her back. "No! No, Tasi, don't go near them."

She lunged again, trying to free herself, but he held her firmly. "I want to see—I want to see her—"

"Her—"

"It must be her!" Tasi said. "It has to be my mother!"

The thought struck Rogett as logical—and then he immediately rejected it.

"No—you can't think that. You can't be sure."

Tasi ceased her struggles. Not once had she taken her eyes from the two figures. "I know—I know. I've felt it from the moment I came in here that I had been here before. I remember. I do—I do—I remember—I was here, do you understand that? This is where I was born and where I was raised—before I was sent down to Kantrell's!"

"No, Tasi, no, you can't be sure. You mustn't think things like that—"

"Murdered," Tasi said at length. Then she calmed down. "They were murdered. You can see that, even you can see they were shot in the back of the head as they slept—"

"You're not even sure who they are. They must have been here for years for their—bodies to decompose to this degree," Rogett said haltingly.

"He did it!" Tasi said bitterly. "He lied! He's done nothing but lie to me all my life! Aahasi and my mother never sent me down to live with him! Why would they do a thing like that? Answer me, Sidney, why would they send me away? He lied. He came up here in the hills and searched until he found them. He probably sneaked in here at night, shot them both and then took me back with him!" Tasi's voice had steadily grown colder, more sure of what she was saying. "Kantrell!" she said at last. "He did it."

Then, as if she could hold it back no longer, she turned and put her head on his chest and sobbed. Her whole body jerked with the violence of her sobs.

Rogett pulled her away gently, turning from the small anteroom of the cave, and walked back toward the opening.

They stood a moment in the harsh sunlight just at the opening, Tasi still in his arms. The sobs lessened and then slowly stopped.

"We will have to bury them, Sidney," she said.

"Of course we will, Tasi," Rogett said tenderly. "I'll get the horse and then we'll look around for a suitable place—"

She nodded and sank from his arms to a boulder and wiped her face with her sleeve. Rogett walked away from the mouth of the cave a short distance, caught the animal and walked it back, his thoughts a jumble, his stomach growling for food, his mouth dry for a drink of water and his eyes sore from the all-night fight against the sand that blew constantly.

"Let's look around inside for a shovel or something we can use to dig with," Rogett said. He brought the horse inside the cave. "Might as well get this fellow out of the sun. Can't give him water, but we can make him as comfortable as possible—"

"Sidney—!" Tasi screamed. "Look!"

He spun around. Tasi was lunging to the interior of the cave and pointing across the canyon floor.

Rogett stared. His eyes saw the movement, but he did not see what it was that moved. Then he did see it.

"Get down! Quickly!" he shouted and pulled at the gun in his waistband.

Meathead's braves were advancing toward the mouth of the cave.

"Watch out!" Tasi screamed and knocked him down a moment before a shaft whistled past his head and bounced back off the far wall of the cave.

Then, like rain, the arrows flew into the opening of the cave and a few seconds later, the increasingly rapid fire of gunshots.

Tasi crawled to the horse, grabbed the leather and pulled the animal back into the anteroom of the cave while Rogett hugged the side walls, inching his way to the rear and taking careful aim at a lean brown body as he returned the fire of the attacking Apaches.

"Here!" Tasi pulled him by the arm and he fell back into the protection of the small partitioning wall.

"Meathead!" Tasi said bitterly. "Well, that old bastard has sure ripped it for good now. When Kantrell finds out that he's come gunning for me, he'll spend the rest of his life until that cunning old devil is cut up with his hair over Kantrell's fireplace."

84

Rogett was only half listening. The arrows and bullets were accurate to the degree that he dared not peek around the corner of the ledge. Again and again the outer inch of the jutting rock was chipped away by bullets and the powerful thrust of iron-tipped arrows.

"Give me the carbine," Tasi said. And Rogett noticed the teeth-clenching determination in her voice. He pulled the carbine down from the saddle boot and handed it to her.

"Careful, Tasi."

"You're the one that needs to be careful," Tasi said. Rogett, after watching Tasi shoot the first few times, relaxed his fears for her safety. She certainly knew how to handle a rifle and she shot with unerring accuracy. She didn't shoot often, but when she did, she hit something. "They're backing off," Tasi said to him.

Rogett looked. There were three bodies visible, sprawled on the canyon floor. Rogett had accounted for one, Tasi had gotten two.

"They won't leave the dead out there," Tasi said. "They'll try and get them before they draw back. Be careful—they'll give us a hell of a lot of trouble as cover for the others that go out and drag the dead ones to one side." Her warning was well taken. As soon as the first head appeared to move out in the open and attempt to get at the dead or wounded, it seemed to Rogett that fifty rifles opened up on them at once and a dozen bowmen let fly their shafts into the opening of the cave. All they could do was drop behind the ledge of rock and wait.

When the firing was over and the rain of arrows had ceased, Rogett dared a glance outside. The ground was clear of the fallen Indians and not a movement could be seen. "They've gone," Rogett said.

"But not for long," Tasi replied. "See that big boulder on the left?"

"Yes."

"They're sitting behind it and working themselves up into a rush at us. If we can stop the rush, they'll leave us alone for a while."

They waited.

Five minutes. Then a half hour. Then an hour. Two hours.

Then three. The cave became unbearably hot. They sipped at the canteen of water sparingly, but they knew there wasn't enough to last them through any prolonged siege. And by now they were both ravenous. Rogett had not eaten for a day and a half and Tasi told him she had taken a little food along with her when she escaped from the ranch. She had only been without food for a day, but she was as hungry as Rogett.

Rogett looked at his watch. It was close to noon.

"How long do you think they'll stay out there and work themselves up?" Rogett asked.

"No telling."

"We won't last long without water—"

"We don't have to worry about that," Tasi said through her clenched teeth. "Here they come—"

The cave exploded with a hundred echoing shots as the Indians poured from behind the rock and ran, shouting, screaming, firing, straight for the cave entrance.

Coolly and effectively, both Tasi and Rogett fired into the first ranks of the oncoming Indians. They saw one, then two—then three—four—five of them fall. But still the line of Indians came forward. They were only a hundred paces from the entrance to the cave when both Tasi and Rogett heard a deep earth-shaking rumble that seemed to come from all around them in the cave. Tasi looked at Rogett. Her expression told him she had no idea what the noise was, or what was causing it.

The Indians heard it then. They skidded to a stop— some of the closer ones only thirty or forty feet away— and began to look up and point. They began to scream, then retreated. As they raced away from the cave, sand and gravel, small stones, then larger stones began to fall at the very mouth of the cave.

Then all at once, while Rogett and Tasi watched, the rockslide covered the entrance to the cave in a matter of seconds. The roar was deafening. The dust and backwash of smaller stones were hurled into the cave with bullet-like force, spraying the inside of the cave with a deadly scatter shot, but the shot was often as big as a man's fist.

In less than a minute the entrance to the cave was sealed off and Rogett and Tasi were in complete darkness.

Tasi began to cough and gag on the clouds of dust that had sifted into the cave. Rogett, himself finding it hard to breathe, and still stunned from a glancing blow from one of the hurtling stones, struggled to his feet gasping for breath. "Tasi! Tasi! Are you all right! Where are you?"

Tasi could not answer right away. Groping around blindly, Rogett found the girl and they stood, both coughing, gasping for breath.

When at last they were able to breathe, Rogett fumbled in his pocket and found a match, struck it and turned at once to the corner where the skeletons had remained undisturbed throughout the resistance against the Indians and the rockslide, found a piece of wood and tried to light it.

"Here!" Tasi said. She had picked up a much smaller stick and had quickly broken it into pieces. The dried twigs caught fire and glowed in the darkness. From this light, Rogett managed to get a strong flame going on the larger stick. They turned to the entrance of the cave.

For ten minutes they examined the top, sides and center of the rockslide that filled the entrance. There was no sign of light, and from Rogett's best judgment, the fall had filled in at least ten feet of the cave, and there was no telling how much was piled up against the side of the hill on the outside.

Sidney Rogett was an engineer, a mining engineer, and all of his professional knowledge and understanding told him that it would take a dozen men a week to get them out.

"It's as tight as a drum," he said.

Tasi began to scream. Rogett was so shocked at first that he only turned and stared at her. But when she screamed a second time he slapped her hard across the face.

"Don't do that again," Rogett said. "If we are to get out of here, we're going to need all the control we can exercise."

In the dimming light of the stick he held aloft, he turned away from the entrance and walked to the back of the cave.

"Come here, Tasi," he said firmly. "While this is still burning, hunt around for more pieces we can use as a torch."

She came forward, stumbling, her black hair falling in her eyes, and began to search the ground. There were only a few pieces of wood.

"Light the largest one," Rogett said. And while Tasi held the second piece of wood near the flame, Rogett turned and looked beyond the two skeletons. He spoke, half to himself, half in hope, with a grim determination. "There must be another way out of here!"

The torch Tasi had lighted flamed up brightly. Rogett dropped the first, stamped on it and took the second from her. "All right, stick close to me," he said.

He held out his hand. She put her own in his and gripped it tightly. Rogett turned his attention to the dark area beyond the bed where the skeletons lay.

Step by step, moving with the hope and the fears of a man who knows full well his situation and the odds against him, Sidney Rogett moved into the darkness, seeing only the few feet of light ahead of him, feeling the pressure of Tasi's hand in his.

Chapter Twelve

THEY HAD NOT GONE FAR when Rogett realized that the walls and ceiling of the cave had begun to close in and down upon them. He could now reach out and touch the side walls and he had to hold the flame lower to keep from touching the top.

Then before him Rogett saw what looked like an opening into a larger room. The walls began to widen, the ceiling grew in height. He quickened his footsteps.

Cautiously they moved through the opening. The flame cast a yellow glow on the surprisingly high walls. The room was nearly twenty feet in diameter and the ceiling thirty feet above their heads.

Rogett looked. He could not believe his eyes. The walls were speckled, as if millions of tiny crystals were flashing, and he knew that he had discovered the greatest gold lode, the mother lode, of the forbidden hills.

But Sidney Rogett did not feel the savage joy that would come with the finding of such a fortune. He passed by the vein, one that covered nearly one whole side of the wall, a vein that he knew would turn out to be one of the richest in America, and searched for a way out.

He made a complete circuit of the room. There was no opening. It was a dead end.

Tasi had followed him. They returned to stand at the entrance. Rogett held the flame high above his head. "There are only a few places in the whole world, Tasi, with a lode like this."

Tasi didn't answer. She wavered on her feet and then as she was about to fall, Rogett dropped the torch and caught her in his arms. "Tasi! Tasi!"

She did not answer. He kneeled down and put her as gently as he could on the ground and began to search for some sign of a wound. He found nothing and then while he was trying to wake her, while his mind searched for some answer to her sudden collapse, she stirred and looked at him. "Water—" she said weakly. "And I'm—I'm hungry—"

Rogett clenched his teeth. "Be still," he said gently. "I'll get the canteen." He started to move away from her.

"No—please don't leave me here!" she cried and half raised herself on her elbow and held out her hand to him. "I'll go with you."

Grimly, their hope of escape fading, they made their way back to the front of the cave. Rogett found the canteen and shook it. He knew there was very little water left, but he said nothing to her. He held the canteen to her lips. Tasi drank quickly, then turned her head away. "Enough," she said weakly.

"You may as well take it now," he heard himself say. "There really isn't any point in saving it, is there?"

"I'm sorry, Sidney," she said weakly.

"Sorry for what?"

"This—"

"Not your fault at all," he said. He slumped down beside her.

"How long do you think—" she began, and then stopped.

"How long do you think we can last?" he asked. "I don't know. Few days at most—without water. If we don't run out of air." She slid her hand into his. He gripped it tightly. "Though there may be some hidden cracks around that we don't know about that would allow a plentiful supply of air."

There were silent for a long time. She moved nearer to him. "The gold—in the back—do you think that was what Aahasi meant—do you think we've found the treasure?"

90

"Yes. That is the treasure," he said.

"The treasure of Aahasi," she repeated softly. "The—treasure—of—Aahasi."

Rogett got up to light another torch. The flames of the new fire lit up the cave, and he walked over to the covered entrance again, examining it carefully, sighed and turned back to her.

"No hope?" she said.

"There must be seventy-five to a hundred tons of earth and rock—" he let his voice trail off.

"Are you married, Sidney?" Tasi asked.

"No."

"Engaged?"

"Yes. In a way."

"Do you love her?"

"I thought so, before I came out here."

"And now?"

"So many things have happened. I can't say."

"Sidney—" she said. And then Tasi raised herself up on her elbow and pulled his head down to hers. She kissed him. She put her arms around his neck and pulled him down, putting her head back down on the ground and then staring up at him in the dim fire light.

"Sidney—" she said again.

Her mouth was hot on his. He tried to collect his reason and pull away from her grasp, but his head began to pound and he found himself kissing in return. She strained her body upwards against him. His hands fumbled with the front of her blouse, opened it and cupped her breast. She shuddered.

Some inner layer of sap that had not dried out in the old piece of wood burst hot and flared brightly, doubling the light in the cave.

Rogett pulled back from her. "Tasi—I—" He turned half away. "We mustn't, Tasi—"

She was not listening to him. She pulled herself upright and stood. Slowly, watching his face, she began stripping off the blouse.

He closed his eyes and turned away.

He heard her footsteps move toward him. She took his chin and pulled it around. "Look at me," she said, her voice husky. "Look at me. You will be the first—and the last—"

She tossed the blouse to one side and began slipping the belt off her skirt, then slowly eased the garment down off her hips and stepped out of it.

She stood before him, the firelight washing her creamy skin in a flickering, wavering light. Her eyes were hooded with half-closed lids, her dark hair was streaming down her back. She slipped down on her knees and fell back into his arms. She pulled his head down and kissed him.

Rogett responded with an energy he did not think was left in him. Her slim young body quivered in response to his touch and kiss. His head pounded.

His thoughts raced wildly. There were snatches of distant thoughts he had had long ago; there were ideas undeveloped that he had hungered to work on; there were sharp, real pictures before his mind's eye of moments in his past life, when he had listened to music at a concert; when he had felt the hush and warmth of his teachers in school when they came near him, the scent of their bodies arousing him; there were wild and insane things that were not connected in any way that he could remember, or that made any sense at all, but that were all tied up with this moment: a beaten girl, an ineffective man in a wild and demanding land that he could not cope with, trapped in a cave.

Then he gave himself over to a harmony and a rhythm that was at once primitive and glorious.

"Tasi—!"

"Sidney, Sidney . . ."

Chapter Thirteen

THE SOUND AT FIRST was that of an animal scratching and Rogett turned on his side. Sleep, exhaustion, hunger and thirst had finally taken hold of him.

He tried to shake the dream off, but it returned.

"Digging," he said half aloud.

Tasi stirred at his side. "Sidney—listen—" she said.

Rogett sat up. The sound came again. The pale red glow of a dying ember was all that prevented them from being in total darkness. "Ssh!" he cautioned as Tasi moved to blow the embers into flame.

The scratching sounds continued, followed by a distant rumble. Not thunderous, but heavy, as if a giant stone had been dislodged and rolled away. The ground shook a little.

A silence, then more of the scratching.

"Someone is digging us out," Rogett said. He waved her back and picked up the carbine, positioned himself, aimed the gun at the top of the rubble and waited.

"What are you doing that for?" Tasi demanded, pointing at the gun.

"Suppose it's Meathead?" he asked.

Tasi had no answer. She retreated to the back of the cave and waited.

The slow, animal-like scratching continued, interrupted from time to time by a thump that Rogett figured to be a huge stone or boulder being rolled down the outside slope of the slide.

An hour passed, then two—then three. Tasi came to

him with the last of the water from the canteen. As time passed, the digging sounds became more definite and Rogett tried to imagine how the digger was working. Probably, he thought, imagining the scene on the outside, whoever it was had started from the top of the slide and dug down to the upper level of the cave opening and then had begun tunneling along the ceiling of the cafe itself. A risky business, he knew. A shifting in the gravel and rock along the sides of the tunnel would trap the digger with no escape.

Another hour passed. The digging sounds never ceased except for brief periods when Rogett knew the digger was hauling away fill from the face of the tunnel. Another hour—then two more.

After the first few hours had passed, Rogett relaxed his guard over the cave. He became aware of another danger now, one that could easily dispel the last faint hope of their survival. The deeper the digger got into the slide, the more dangerous became his position and the greater the possibility of the side walls falling in on him.

"How long has it been now?" Tasi asked him.

Rogett looked at his watch. "About twelve hours since we first heard it," he replied.

"I wonder who it is?" Tasi said, asking herself the question.

"I hope we get a chance to find out," Rogett replied.

The digging sounds continued, hour after hour, and getting louder and louder.

"Why is it taking him so long?" Tasi asked.

"The deeper he gets, the longer the tunnel is and the longer it is for him to haul away what he digs out. And he has to be careful there won't be a cave-in on him."

"Why don't you get some sleep?" she asked.

"What's the point?" he asked, touching her face. "If he makes it, I don't want to be sleeping—and if he doesn't, there will be plenty of time to—"

She put her fingers over his lips. "Don't—" she whispered.

"Are you frightened?"

"I was at first. But now—I'm not sure."

"The odds are fantastic against whoever it is doing the digging," he said.

They lapsed into silence. They had not bothered to re-light their torch and now sat in total darkness. Tasi fell asleep with her head resting on Rogett's lap and he began to count the regular breathing, fighting against sleep himself, exhausted from the lack of food and water.

He jerked upright, suddenly. He shivered. There was a noise, a falling rock near his foot.

Tasi was awake, lifting her head, and instantly Rogett put his hand over her mouth. They remained perfectly still.

Rogett shivered again. There was a definite movement of air. Then he located the draft. It was coming from above him.

Tasi eased from his lap and Rogett stood, stiffly, and moved cautiously. The blast of air from the top of the slag heap was quite strong and he knew that whoever had been digging had opened the tunnel. "Ssh!" he warned Tasi. "I'm going up."

Following the draft of chilling air, Rogett wondered why he could not see light and then he understood as his hands found the top of the cave and the opening. He gazed through. The darkness of the cave was not as dark as that of the night outside.

He waited, straining every fiber of his being for some sound that would reveal something of what might be going on outside.

He waited for five minutes—then five more. He heard nothing. "Tasi!" he called softly. "Come up. But be careful you don't dislodge anything!"

She moved with care up to his side. They both heard a noise coming through the tunnel at the same time. "What was that?" she asked.

Rogett had already decided what he was going to do. "Whatever is out there, knew we were in here and took a dangerous chance to dig us out. Come on."

He moved toward the opening that was not much

wider than his shoulders. "Crawl slowly, keep your head well down and move along on your elbows and toes. Don't hurry. Don't panic. If you get frightened, lie flat, face down and wait until you have control of yourself, then move on the same way. Elbows pulling you along, toes kicking you forward."

"Yes—" Tasi said and he heard the strength come into her voice.

He moved into the tunnel, inching the carbine along at his side. He had moved in about eight feet when he stopped and lay flat. "Tasi—are you coming?"

She touched his boot. "Yes. Right behind you."

"All right, no more talking now. Let's go."

It did not take them long to scrape their elbows raw, but they continued to move steadily, an inch at a time, moving only their elbows to drag them forward, then kicking ahead with their toes. The crawl seemed an eternity. Rogett had tried to keep an estimate of his forward progress by counting three inches for each move forward of his elbows, but he stopped counting and concentrated on control. The pain in his elbows became overwhelming and only the thought that Tasi was suffering the same thing kept him from crying out or pausing. The force of air in the tunnel became stronger as they approached the end. Soon he was able to see the difference between the darkness of the tunnel and the light that kept the outside night blue-black.

He forced his hands up before him, found the outer edge of the tunnel and pulled gently. He was halfway out of the tunnel, flat on the side of the slag heap of rubble, and then free altogether. He turned and reached in for Tasi's hand, grabbed it and helped her out.

She stood, weeping, and then raised her bruised and bleeding elbows, then flung her arms around his neck. Rogett stood close to her, his arms around her.

"Darling—" he said.

He felt her stiffen in his arms. He did not have to turn to see the dancing shadows a flame might throw on the side of the heap. He turned slowly, brought up the carbine and threw a shell into the chamber. Around one side of the cave entrance, there was the glow of a fire—then he heard the snap of a twig.

He moved to the side, dropped down to the ground and eased up to the edge. He poked the barrel of the carbine over the side and sighted down on the fire.

Nothing moved. He could see two Indian ponies hobbled to one side. There was a rabbit being roasted on a spit over the dying fire. A canteen of water lay beside the fire.

He waited. The darkness of the canyon floor was hushed, and without sound. Not a thing moved. There was no sign of anyone.

Tasi was at his side now, looking over his shoulder. "What is it?" he asked, once she had seen the fire and the situation.

"I don't see anything," Tasi said.

He slipped the carbine into her hands. "I'm going to run toward the fire—stomp it out and then dive into the darkness on the other side. Cover me."

"Please—!" she hesitated.

"Don't worry," he assured her. He set himself and waited, he did not know for what. Suddenly Rogett was seized with an uncontrollable urge to laugh. It was madness. It was all a fantastic nightmare that he would wake up to and be frightened of for a few moments and then go back to sleep in his bed in Boston. He, Sidney Rogett, looking at the seared carcass of a rabbit as if it were the only thing left in the world.

Then he lunged. He didn't know just exactly when, but he found himself racing, half stumbling, half falling toward the fire. He kicked at the almost burnt-out flickering light and spread the sparks, stamped on the largest of them that still flamed and then dove for the darkness, his boot catching the rabbit and sending it to the ground.

He lay still. The Indian ponies moved, made a noise and then settled. Nothing moved. He told himself he would wait five minutes before he moved. That would be

97

a slow count of three hundred.

He began.

One hundred—two hundred—two hundred and fifty—

Then he heard Tasi's voice. "Sidney—!"

He pulled her down beside him and took the rifle. "Did you see anything? Anything at all?" he demanded.

"Nothing."

"Are you sure?" he grabbed her arm and she let out a moan of pain. "*Did you see anything?*"

"Noth—nothing—Sidney! What's the matter?"

"Stay here!" he commanded. He crawled off into the darkness and scrambled around, burning his hands on the hot coals he had scattered and returned a moment later with the rabbit that was roasting hot and covered with grit, and the canteen. "Here, water, drink slowly and don't take too much." He kept his head moving, turning.

"Sidney—you sound—what is it?"

"Drink!" he commanded.

She took the canteen and drank. When she had taken a few swallows, he pulled the canteen away from her roughly. He took a short swallow himself, screwed the cap back on the top and slung it over his shoulder. He removed his shirt, rolled the rabbit in it and tucked it under his arm.

"Now crawl toward the horses," he said, his voice carrying the same harshness as before. "We're getting the hell away from here."

"But Sidney—"

"*Move!*" he said.

"Where will we go in the darkness?" Tasi pleaded. "We can't see. We can't ride off—the horses will stumble."

She reached out and touched his cheek. "Darling—what is it? Why are you behaving this way? We're free—we're out. I don't know who did it, but—"

"Listen to me," Rogett said, gripping her shoulders. "I haven't been in your country long. But I've been here long enough to learn one thing: Death comes quickly and it comes in many forms. Life out here is for the man

98

who takes precautions. If there is one thing I've learned, it's to take precautions. Things have happened to me in the last three or four days—I don't know how long it has been—that have made me a little insane, I guess, I don't know. People wanting to kill me. Wild savages attacking me. Men that plan to steal my money. Crazy stories about a woman and an Indian. And a king's ransom of treasure in a cave that—that has two skeletons inside with bullet holes in the back of their skulls—and then this! Someone works—*works*, Tasi, I know, because I'm a mining engineer—hours, taking a dangerous chance with each handful of earth he moves, or each rock he takes out, of being trapped himself in a cave-in—all this to get us out, and then when we're out—we find a fire, a roasting rabbit—and a canteen of water and two horses—"

Tasi was crying. "I know, darling—I know—I know—"

"No—you don't know! You don't know, because you've been brought up to believe all this mystery business about your mother and father—whoever he may be—raised to believe that it's true. It's not true, Tasi, it's a lie. A dirty, terrible, bitter lie that someone is in back of, for what reason I don't know. But I tell you this. Two things. I love you: and I'm going to find out what the hell this is all about. I've had enough. *Enough!* From now on, I'm going to play the game just as roughly and just as mysteriously and just as deadly. If it's killing they want, I'll give it to them. I'm tired of running."

He took a deep breath. "Now get on one of those horses. You lead the way. We'll stop somewhere else. I'm right behind you, but don't get too far ahead of me, because I'm going to kill anything that moves, Indian or white man."

Chapter Fourteen

IT WAS TASI that discovered the Indian sign the next morning. A crude pile of stones in the form of an arrow pointing in a direction that would take them over the top of the forbidden hills. They had finished the last of the rabbit and were about to move out of the little clearing they had found refuge in for the night when the discovery was made.

"What does it mean?" Rogett asked. Both were on the ground examining the stones.

"Indian signs for marking a trail."

"For us?" Rogett asked.

"I don't know. It may be," Tasi said. She examined the stones more closely. "There isn't much sand packed around the bottom of the rocks—indicating they might have been here a while." She stood up suddenly and began to search the area.

She stopped and pointed to a slight depression in the ground. "This is where they got the rocks. The ground underneath the rock is still a little damp. And there is hardly any drift sand in it. I'd say that the sign was made sometime last night."

"Then our mysterious helper is providing us with a way out of these damn hills," Rogett said, glancing around.

They followed the sign, with Tasi in the lead, moving upward again toward the high rims of the hills. They came upon another sign at a twist in the trail and didn't pick up another until they had reached the top. A third sign pointed along the ridge and they followed it, taking a route that seemed unlikely, but proved to be the only way down the opposite side. They stopped once to give the horses a breather and took a drink of water, and by noon they were well down the opposite side of the hills and could see the flats below them.

They didn't see any more signs, but it was unnecessary. Tasi knew the country well from there on in. "Straight across that flat," she said, "then toward the west and we'll hit the main road into town."

Rogett said nothing.

"We should be there by mid-afternoon," Tasi said, looking at Rogett in a strange way. She looked as if she wanted to ask him something, but then changed her mind.

They rode out of the hills, seeing no one and no movement of any kind, moving steadily across the wide sandy flats. They did not ride too fast: the heat would not allow that. The sun was broiling.

Several times Tasi turned to look at Rogett as if she wanted to ask a question, but then stopped. If Rogett had seen her face, he might have anticipated her question, but his thoughts were not of the girl at the moment, but of what he might find in Jicarilla.

Rogett had always tried to anticipate the moves of his opponents, whether in business or games; he found a certain sense of the contest to be satisfying and often, whether he succeeded or lost, was rewarded with a feeling of satisfaction for having been in a challenge. But for the first time in his life, he found that he was not thinking about the contest, the challenge, or what might be done against him: he was thinking about what he was going to do, how he could move to insure success. He had learned and adopted this attitude in the short time that he had been in that part of the country: strike hard, strike first, strike to win, with no thought for the methods used or the feelings of his challenger.

He did not notice Tasi's questioning eyes or the sudden gasp of breath that would warn him she was about

101

to say something because he was working out the groundwork for instant success. There was only one thing that Sidney Rogett wanted now. He wanted to marry Tasi and to unlock the question of Jezebel. The question of Jezebel in itself did not interest him. What did interest him was why his life had been placed in jeopardy —and why someone had saved his life.

They did not allow the heat to stop them and pushed the ponies on until they were well off the burning flats and on the road to Jicarilla.

They moved past small buildings, saw a few people; a few riders passed them going in the opposite direction but they did not stop, did not return the greetings of the strangers.

They rode into Jicarilla a little before four that afternoon, swung up the main street and pulled up before the Western Hotel. They did not appear to notice the stares and the whispering of the townsfolk that stopped to watch the strange couple.

The clerk at the desk looked up, eyes bugging out at the sight of the man and the woman, hardy able to recognize Sidney Rogett with a heavy growth of beard, filthy clothes, wild hair, and the girl beside him that looked nearly as bad as he did. But he did recognize them after a moment. "Good God Almighty!" he breathed. "Mister Rogett! Tasi Kantrell! What—"

"Two rooms," Rogett said, his cold voice just a shade short of being hard. "One for Miss Kantrell, one for myself. We will both want baths, of course."

The clerk paled. "Mister Rogett—I've got a room ready and you can be in the bathtub in five minutes. But—" he looked at Tasi. "I can't do a thing for Miss Tasi."

"Why not?" Rogett demanded in the same cold voice.

"Mister Rogett—you've just got to understand—I've been warned not to help Miss Tasi in any way."

Rogett raised the carbine, cocked it and placed the barrel flat on the desk, aimed at the clerk's heart. "Now you're getting another warning," he said. "Two rooms, two baths."

The clerk looked at Tasi. "Please, Miss Tasi, you know how Betajack is when he gets mad—and your father. He'll give it to me—"

"If you don't give me two rooms with two baths by the time I count three, sir," Rogett said. "It won't be Betajack, nor Kantrell, but myself that will give it to you."

The clerk made one last appealing look toward Tasi and then sighed. "Yes, sir. Right away, Mister Rogett."

"And have some clean clothes brought to the rooms. A selection both for myself and Miss Kantrell," Rogett said. He had not removed the gun from the desk, nor the aim away from the clerk's heart. "The best there is in town."

"Yes, sir. Right away, sir. But when Betajack 'r Mister Kantrell comes in, will you explain that you had a gun on me when—"

"Do your own explaining," Rogett said coldly. "The rooms."

"Twenty-two for you and forty-one for Miss Tasi." The clerk pointed toward the head of the stairs.

At the top of the stairs, Rogett stopped Tasi. "How long will it take for a rider to get out to the ranch and return?"

"At least four hours." Tasi replied. "Why?"

"Then we have that much time before we can expect a visitor."

"Sidney—" Tasi said.

"Yes?"

Tasi pulled back. "Never mind." She walked away quickly, found her room and entered. Rogett stood a moment, thinking about her unasked question. While he stood, two young boys began to struggle up the stairs with a bathtub. Following them was an old Mexican woman tottering under the weight of two steaming buckets of water. Rogett pointed toward Tasi's door and then watched while the tub was taken inside. The boys came out and the old woman stayed in.

"It'll only be a minute, mister," one said.

"Bring a razor," Rogett instructed, turned and walked

103

into his room. It was not long before the two boys returned, wrestling with a second metal tub. Rogett watched them both, decided on the younger one that looked like he might be about twelve. He stopped him at the door. He held out a twenty-dollar gold piece. "I want to know the minute anyone from the Kantrell ranch comes into town. And I want to know where they are and what they're doing. Another one just like this is yours if you're accurate."

The boy looked at the gold coin, licked his lips. He hesitated. "Are you afraid?" Rogett asked.

"No, sir. That ain't it."

"What is it?"

"I don't know what accurate means."

Rogett found himself smiling for the first time in what seemed like weeks. "Accurate, in this case, son, means telling me the truth and being sure of what you tell me."

"I can do that, mister," the boy said.

Rogett gave him the gold piece.

"Remember, the minute anyone from the Kantrell ranch comes into town—where they are and what they're doing."

"Yes, sir."

"And no one is to know that you're doing this. *No one!*"

"Mister, for that much money, I wouldn't tell the Lord Jesus how to get back into heaven," the boy said soberly.

Rogett burst out laughing. "Very well."

He closed the door, checked the carbine and began to undress.

Chapter Fifteen

"THEY'RE HERE, MISTER," the boy said.

A group of men were watching Rogett as he and Tasi stopped at the bottom of the stairs, clean and fresh in the new clothes.

"How many?" Rogett asked, stiffening.

"Jest two of them. Mister Queen, and an old man they call Skunk."

"Where are they?"

"Saloon across the street called the Aces," the boy said. "They're over there now having themselves a drink."

"Has Queen said anything?" Rogett asked. The group of men in the hotel lobby moved in closer to hear the conversation. "Well?" Rogett pressed when the boy hesitated.

"He said a lot of things—" the boy looked at Tasi. "But you'd slap me down for saying them in front of her."

"All right, son," Rogett said. "Here's your money." He gave the boy a double eagle.

The boy took the money and then looked at Rogett. "You going to do any shooting with Mister Queen?"

"Why?"

"Well, you don't look like much with a gun," the boy said thoughtfully. "And since you and me are kinda friends, I thought I'd tell you it would be a damn sight better if you went in shooting first. Mister Queen done allowed to anyone that would listen that he figures to take you apart piece by piece."

The boy moved away. So did the group of men that

had heard. There weren't many in Jicarilla that wanted any part of a man that was going to buck Kantrell—and start if off by facing up to Betajack Queen.

"Coming, Tasi?"

"He'll kill you," Tasi said. "You don't know him—"

"I know enough."

"Please, send for horses and—"

"Do you want to run?"

"Yes—"

"They'll catch you. And you'll go back to the Kantrell ranch and it will be worse than it was before."

"I don't care," Tasi said. "Please, Sidney—"

Rogett walked her through the lobby to the doorway. They stood alone. The street was nearly deserted. At the sight of Rogett and Tasi, those that were moving about the street disappeared into the nearest doorway. Rogett felt the chilling isolation of the moment. It was more than just being alone in the forbidden hills, or trapped in the cave. Those moments had been not of his choosing.

But this decision was his own. Made consciously, overtly, knowing full well what the measures were.

It wasn't that Kantrell and Betajack had tried to swindle him out of a half million dollars, Rogett thought as they walked out of the hotel into the street. Nor was it the attempts on his life.

He could not, accurately, say to himself what was motivating him. But he knew he had changed—a change that had come gradually, slowly, from the inner core of the man.

Sidney Rogett was very aware that he was tasting his first trail of courage. As a man. It was a new dimension for him. There were no recourses to law, friends, moral codes. Here it was. Man to man.

It was a deeply personal thing, and he knew that he would never be able to return to the East and his life there, dealing with problems, facing them, without the encouragement of having faced this problem now, on its own terms. He would never be able to marry Tasi and

106

take her with pride back to the East knowing that he had walked away from a fight.

So the change had come. As subtle as the changes in climate, as mysterious as the soul of the man himself.

They were across the street now. The eyes of men and women watched their movement across the street from hidden corners and through half-drawn curtains. There weren't many in Jicarilla that didn't know, by then, that Betajack Queen was on the warpath for Sidney Rogett. And those that did not know, were soon told—and recognized Tasi Kantrell.

They stepped onto the boardwalk and started down toward the door of the saloon when the doors opened and Skunk appeared.

"God Almighty!" he said softly and hurried toward them. "You two younguns all right?"

"Where is Queen?" Rogett demanded.

"Inside, standing at the bar."

Rogett started to push past him. Skunk grabbed his arm. "What you aiming to do?"

"Get some answers."

"You ever fit with a gun before?"

"You going to try and stop me, old man?" Rogett said harshly.

"Not me!" Skunk said, backing up. "I'll just stay out here with Miss Tasi and dodge the lead. You go right on in, Mist' Rogett. Step right on inside."

"Sidney—please!" Tasi reached for his arm. "We can still get away. Skunk will help us—"

Rogett looked at the old man. "It seems that Skunk tried to help us once before." Skunk dropped his eyes.

Rogett turned and walked into the saloon. He paused at the entrance and looked around. The room was three-quarters filled. Men were drinking or playing cards. The drinkers and the card players paused to look up at the newcomer, and then seeing who it was, stopped their activity cold.

Queen saw Rogett's reflection in the mirror behind the bar. He turned slowly as Rogett approached. "Well, well,

well! Look what we got here—managed to crawl into town, did you? Where's Tasi?"

Queen's voice was harsh and demanding and had the authoritative command that Rogett recognized.

Rogett did not answer. He held Queen's gaze. Queen pushed away from the bar and took a step forward. "You got a rifle," Queen stated.

Rogett maintained his silence.

"Planning on using it?"

Rogett said nothing.

Queen walked around Rogett slowly, speaking, talking to the men in the bar, playing off Rogett. "A goddamn no-account Easterner that can't even wipe his own nose. I ast you a goddamn question, now answer me before I git good and mad. Where's Miss Tasi?"

Rogett turned slowly. He did not let his eyes stray from Queen's face. He turned slowly, raising the rifle, and held it straight out, pointing at the door and street. "She's right outside."

Then he swung his body back again, bringing the barrel of the carbine around with all the strength and speed he could manage. Queen saw the blow coming and made one mistake. He went for his gun instead of trying to dodge the blow. The barrel of the carbine caught him at the temple before he had drawn his gun clear of the holster. There was a sickening thud and Betajack Queen slumped to the floor, out cold.

Rogett leaned down and slipped the heavy Colt out of the man's hand and stuck it into his waistband. Skunk appeared at the door with Tasi. He walked into the dead silence of the room and stared at Queen. He looked up at Rogett. He shook his head from side to side. "You're learning might quick," Skunk said. "Yessir, might-tee quick! You'll do, Mist' Rogett."

Rogett turned to the room full of watchful, waiting, silent men, still a little stunned that Betajack Queen had been taken. Slowly, Rogett stared into the face of each man. When he spoke, there was a harsh, absolute conviction that none could mistake.

"I'm hiring men," he said. "A hundred dollars a day in gold. Men with guns who are not afraid to use them. Men that are sick and tired of being dominated by Kantrell and his hired thugs. One hundred dollars a day in gold. I'm riding against Kantrell in the morning."

Silence.

Rogett turned and took Tasi by the arm. They walked out of the saloon. Behind them, Rogett heard the silence broken by Skunk's loud roar. "You heard the man. A hunnert a day in gold. Ain't one of you that ain't got something against Kantrell and been belly-aching about wishing something could be done—well, here's your chance. One hunnert dollars a day in gold—and you all know me well enough to abide what I say. I say Mist' Rogett done proved he's a man with what he done to old Betajack here on the floor. Any man with the gumption to do that, *and* pay a hunnert dollars a day to boot, has got me and my gun."

Rogett did not know until the next morning that he had hired twenty-one men and that they had taken Queen and sent him unarmed back to the Kantrell ranch.

Chapter Sixteen

THE FILE OF MEN had been riding since daybreak, raising a high trail of dust all the way from Jicarilla to the Kantrell ranch. It was not Rogett's plan to surprise Kantrell. He only wanted a show of force, since force was necessary to have what was rightfully his, returned. He hoped to avoid bloodshed, but he was prepared for it.

He rode alone at the head of the column of twos, with Tasi and Skunk right behind him. More than once Skunk had ridden to his side and pointed to something Skunk identified as an Indian sign.

"Meathead is still out. And he's still after hair."

Rogett had not replied. But the men behind him knew the signs as well as Skunk and they were careful, watching the sun side of the trail, talking, making comment to each other in low, tense voices.

They were only a half mile from the Kantrell ranch when Skunk moved up alongside of Rogett. "What you aiming to do when we git there, Mist' Rogett?"

"Get some answers."

Skunk deliberated a long time about this. "To what kind of questions?"

"You'll hear them."

"Might be that I can answer some of them for you."

Rogett turned and looked at the old man. "I don't think so, Skunk."

Skunk was about to press the point when they both saw a rider beating back up the trail toward them.

Rogett pulled up the carbine, but Skunk's hand went

out to warn him away. "It's one of Kantrell's men," he said.

"What could he want?"

"Skunk," Tasi said, coming up along side of them, "isn't that Hank?"

"Yup," Skunk said.

They watched the rider coming toward them, raising dust and waving his hat. He was still some distance away when they could hear him screaming. The one word made the clammy sweat break out on each man's neck.

Rogett didn't hear it clearly enough to recognize the word, but Skunk heard it, and so did Tasi. "What's he saying?" Rogett demanded.

"Indians!" Skunk said.

And then the man was on them.

"It's Meathead—it's Meathead!" the man yelled. "He's cutting up the ranch—and already set fire to the bunk-house—"

Skunk grabbed the man's leather and jerked the nervous horse to a standstill, holding the animal down tightly. "Now, just hold on, Hank!" he said. "What the hell is this all about?"

The man was sweating, his face was grime-covered and streaked. "He hit us about an hour before dawn. We didn't know thing about it. Betajack came back madder'n hell about the Easterner giving him a rousting in town, and he was inside talking to Mister Kantrell most of the night. He just happened to be walking back over to the bunkhouse when he saw them sneaking in and gave the alarm, otherwise we'd have been burnt to a crisp! How many men you got here?"

"How come we don't hear no shooting going on?" Skunk demanded. "We close enough for that?"

"They stopped about a half hour ago—and that was when I sneaked out. I was heading for town to get help—" Then the sudden realization that he had found a small army of men on the way to the ranch occurred to him.

"What the hell you all doing out here, Skunk?"

"We were heading for the ranch."

"Well come on—I'll lead the way—"

"No you don't," Skunk said. "Not so fast."

"What's the matter?" Hank demanded.

"We ain't riding into a fight that's already going on."

"Just a minute, Skunk," Rogett said. "I don't think that's for you to decide."

Skunk had his gun out and was aiming it at Hank. "Mist' Rogett, I'm going to prove something to you." He raised the gun and fired it over his head. The echo of the shot rolled back and forth in the hills, echoing and re-echoing a half dozen times. "You can hear a shot fired in these hills for miles. That's one reason why I think this feller is a liar. Another is that we're close enough to see some smoke from that bunkhouse fire that was supposed to have been set, but we don't see nothing."

The man licked his lips nervously. "I'm telling you the truth, Skunk. I wouldn't lie to you—"

"Like hell you wouldn't!" Skunk said, and brought the barrel of his gun down hard on the man's head. Hank slipped out of his saddle and fell to the ground. Skunk put his gun away and turned to Rogett. "They're probably sitting around waiting for us to ride in like soljers and roust out Meathead, and then they'll cut us down," Skunk said. "Well, this youngun ain't about to get suckered into a thing like that, if you don't mind, Mist' Rogett."

"We're riding in," Rogett said. "Indians or no Indians."

"But that's plain goddamn foolishness," Skunk insisted.

"Would you have me turn around and go back?" Rogett asked.

Skunk looked at Tasi, then at Rogett. "If you was to ask me that, I would have to say yes. It don't make sense, a man walking into a trap that he knows is there."

"You're being paid a hundred dollars a day—just like the others," Rogett said. "You are free to quit, if that's the way you feel."

Rogett turned in his saddle and spoke to the men that had moved in around them. "If there are any others that feel the way Skunk feels, you can turn back now. But you knew what the job was when you took it."

He waited. The men looked at one another. No one moved.

"All right," Rogett said. "Let's go on in."

Rogett moved away from the others and on down the trail. One by one the men slipped past Skunk and rode after Rogett.

Tasi and Skunk were left standing alone. She looked at him. "I don't want him killed, Skunk—" she said. Her eyes filled with tears.

"Well, he's sure as hell going to git kilt, if someone don't take care of him. That man's got sand, and more than a share of grit, but you got hell and high water when you got sand and grit and no sense. Come on!" He slapped at the horse and the two of them broke down the trail after the others.

Skunk pulled up along side of Rogett. Neither man looked at the other for a while. They were well along the last few hundred yards that would take them into the open area of the ranch buildings when Skunk spoke to him. "If you'd listen to somebody that knows, you'd send in a talker."

"A talker?"

"Someone to make pow-wow with Kantrell. Might be you could save a lot of these feller's lives." He jerked his thumb back of his shoulder at the column of men. "Most of them ain't never had a hundred dollars at one time in their whole life and they ain't quite right in their heads thinking about what they're doing."

Rogett stopped his horse.

Skunk licked his lips. "Can't send in a talker though, until the talker knows what he's going to pow-wow about. What terms are you asking? What do you want?"

"You're suggesting that I send you?"

"Well, I know Queen and Kantrell. I know how to talk

113

to them. I know when they're lying and when they ain't. I know when to trust them and when not to."

"What are you getting out of all this, Skunk?" Rogett asked suddenly.

"What do you mean?"

"Just what I said." Rogett repeated the question again. "What are you getting out of this?"

"Why—the satisfaction of seeing Betajack get his'n, and maybe—well, Kantrell's been high and mighty a long time—"

"Don't lie to me, old man!" Rogett said.

"Mister, you're the simplest minded idjut I ever met up with. You just don't know nothing."

"Answer my goddamn question!" Rogett said, and he threw a shell into the chamber of the carbine and aimed at Skunk's stomach. "First you promise to help me and Tasi, and then you leave me out on the flats alone. You tell me you're through with Kantrell and then when Tasi and I finally get into Jicarilla, you show up with Queen. Now you're back helping me again, and getting that long nose of yours over-extended and into my affairs—now, for the last time, I'm asking you, *what is your interest in this?*"

"My, you sure remind me of that yummy-mouthed feller down to Lane County—"

Rogett raised the rifle. There was a rush of hoof-beats and Tasi rode in, breaking her hand down over the barrel of the rifle. "Look!" she pointed to the rear of them.

"Lord save us on what be this our dying day!" Skunk said. A thousand yards in back of them the trail was filled with the horses and the half-naked bodies of Meathead's Apaches.

"Get to the ranch!" Tasi yelled to the others. "Run—"

The column broke out into a mad gallop for the protection of the ranch.

The force that Rogett had collected in Jicarilla broke full into the open area before the ranch buildings and

114

was immediately met with a round of fire. Several horses were hit, throwing their riders to the ground. Others rode on into the fire coming from the ranch house and the out-buildings, yelling and pointing over their shoulders.

Meatheard was pounding hard on their trail when the column had broken and scrambled for cover and Kantrell's shots paused a moment, the steady stream of fire hesitating on seeing the force that Rogett had brought with him, obviously not concentrating on returning the fire, but more concerned with what was behind them.

Then all at once the whole area was filled with Apaches. They rode through, making one pass at the buildings and the men that had not yet found cover, and riding on to pull up just beyond range of the men inside the buildings.

Six men lay on the ground. Several horses had been hit, some by the Apaches, some by Kantrell's men. The screams of the injured horses and men filled the bright morning air.

Skunk and Rogett and several others had found temporary shelter behind a wagon, but they knew that it would not do for another drive from Meathead's angry braves.

"We got to get inside that house, Mist' Rogett," Skunk said. "Now if there was ever a time for talking, it's now. You better get Kantrell for a talk and get these men you brought out here under cover, or everyone of 'em will be dead 'fore noon."

Rogett looked around the area. His men were down behind dead horses, some of them were trying to find shelter around the sides of the buildings. He did not see Tasi anywhere. Skunk was right. He had to get the men inside. Already the fire from the buildings, a moment before concentrated on the Indians, was being turned on the men in the clearing.

"Kantrell!" Rogett bellowed. "Kantrell—can you hear me?"

There was a pause, the shooting stopped. A moment later, Rogett could hear Kantrell's voice. "Yeah—I hear you."

"These men have got to have cover!" Rogett said. "The next time the Indians come through there won't be one of them left alive!"

"That's their—" The last words were lost.

Rogett turned to Skunk. "What did he say?"

"I don't know."

Rogett turned to the house again. "We'll all die, if you don't let us inside, Kantrell!" Rogett screamed. "They'll get us, and then they'll burn you out—together we can beat them off."

Skunk nodded. "That's right."

There was a little shooting between the men in the houses and Rogett's men outside, but it was only half-hearted.

"Rogett!" Kantrell's voice cut through the random fire again. "You hear me?"

"Go ahead!" Rogett yelled back.

"Bring your men inside—we'll have our fight out afterwards!"

Rogett looked at Skunk. "Can we trust him?"

" 'Pears to this youngun that you ain't got a hell of a big choice," Skunk said. "And besides, them men inside and the men outside, whatever their likes and dislikes, they don't cotton to seeing white man layed up and open by Injuns."

Rogett made his decision. He looked around the area. He signaled the men to stop their firing and move out into the open.

He stepped out first. The hair on the back of his neck began to stiffen. He felt the sweat run down the length of his legs and into his boots.

Gingerly, the rifle at his side, Sidney Rogett walked out and saw that his men were also slipping out of their makeshift cover and walking toward the house.

Not a shot was fired. Suddenly there was an explosive

roar and Rogett turned to see one of his men putting a bullet through the brain of his wounded and fallen horse. The wounded men were picked up and carried into the ranch house. The last of the men were hurrying across the yard when Skunk's cry filled the air.

"Here they come agin!"

Chapter Seventeen

IT WAS NO CONTEST for the Indians. The unusually heavy, concentrated fire of the many guns in the house worked the attacking Indians over manfully.

The air inside the house was filled with smoke and the sound of men pumping shells into chambers, or grunting a satisfying grunt when their shot connected or when there was a near miss.

Rogett knelt at the window beside Kantrell. They said nothing. They did not look at each other. But Rogett had seen Queen when he rushed into the building and noted briefly and with some satisfaction that the ramrod had a thick white bandage around his head.

He did not look for Tasi. He had seen her go into the house with the first of the men after the truce with Kantrell and knew that she was somewhere in the house. It was enough for him at the moment.

A third attack came. Then a fourth. Then there was a long pause of nearly a half hour. During this time, Tasi and the Spanish woman came out with coffee, meat and bread. Tasi served Rogett coffee and smiled at him.

Kantrell did not miss the smile. He looked at Rogett. "You shot three that I could count," he said to Rogett without looking at him, turning his head away quickly.

"Four," Rogett said.

"Well, I only counted three," Kantrell said. "It's a damn good thing you came along when you did."

Rogett said nothing.

Another attack was coming on. If it was to be the last,

as some of the men in the room seemed to think, it would surely be the most pressing. Rogett shot a brave only three feet from the window, catching the man in the chest, but not killing him. Kantrell put a bullet in the Indian's head.

"You're the cause of all this," Kantrell said. "Meathead was a good Indian until you had to go and kill his son."

"He should have taught his son not to shoot at other people," Rogett said coldly.

"I might have expected you to say something like that."

The conversation stopped. The fighting with the Indians had fallen off now. Rogett was struck with the amazingly small percentage of hits the men in the ranch house had made. He had himself killed five, or at least he had hit five of the Indians, and after the hundreds—thousands—of shots fired, he wondered how it was possible for any of the Indians to be left alive.

It was nearly noon when Kantrell shouted, "There he is. It's old Meathead himself and he wants to talk."

"About what?" Rogett asked.

"I'm going out to find out."

"I'll go with you," Rogett said.

"No, you don't, you sit right where you are, mister. You've caused enough trouble."

The men in the room were silent. They were watching, listening.

Rogett stood up. "I said," Rogett spoke with a voice that was equal to that of Kantrell's, "that I'm going with you."

"You *ain't!*"

Rogett walked to the door. He opened it, throwing it back and standing exposed in the open. "Skunk!" he called.

"Here!"

"You speak their language?"

"Sure—but Mist' Kantrell does too—"

"Goddamn you—!" Kantrell said. He started to raise his gun. But Rogett had held the rifle aimed at the man the whole time.

119

"You pull that trigger, Kantrell, and you'll die right where you stand."

"You don't know what the hell he wants!" Kantrell shouted. He pointed at Meathead and three of his braves standing in the middle of the yard, waiting. "He wants *you*—he wants the man that killed his son!"

Rogett looked at Skunk. "Is that true?"

"Probably."

"What does that mean?"

"It means—that it's true."

"And what happens if he doesn't get the man that killed his son?"

"Keeps fighting. Probably bring up flame arrows and burn us out. Then when we come out, get us one at a time," Skunk said, and there was something about the way he said it that made Rogett believe him.

Tasi came and held his arm. "Let Kantrell and Skunk handle it. They can say one of the dead men was the one that killed his son and maybe he'll go away satisfied."

Rogett nodded. "All right."

Kantrell and Skunk slipped through the door. The men moved to the windows to watch. They could see Skunk and Kantrell talking to the old man, who in turn spoke to his braves. There was a disagreement. Meathead shook his head. The braves began to shout and point toward the house.

"What is it?" Rogett asked Tasi.

"I'll tell you," a voice said at his side. "They want a live one. They want one that they can play with a long time before he dies. They don't believe that one of the dead ones is the one that killed his son."

It was Betajack Queen. He was smiling.

Skunk and Kantrell walked back toward the ranch house, both frowning. They entered the room, stooped over and picked up their guns.

"He wouldn't buy the story about one of the dead cowboys being the one that killed his son," Skunk said. "He wants a live one—to play with."

Kantrell nodded in agreement.

120

"One of us!" Queen said. "Meathead wants *him!*" He pointed at Rogett.

Rogett clenched his teeth. Here it was. He was in it. He, Sidney Rogett from Boston. He had killed a savage Indian's son and he was to be handed over in return.

All eyes in the room were turned to Rogett. "What does it mean?" he asked in a firm, clear voice.

"They'll kill you—nice and slow," Queen said.

"No—no—!" Tasi said. "I won't let it happen!" She raised her gun and aimed it at Queen. "*You* go!"

Queen said soberly, "Put that gun down, Tasi. This is no joke. This man killed Meathead's son and he's got to pay for it. The man that walks through that door is as good as dead. He did it, let him pay the debt."

Rogett looked at Tasi. The room was against him. But did it matter? He couldn't let another man go in his place.

"What happens," he asked, for he was not going to throw his life away foolishly, "what happens if we continue to fight?"

"They'll burn us out and every one of us will be dead before the sun goes down," Queen said. "But you needn't think about that, Rogett, because you're going out there and take your medicine."

Rogett didn't say a word. He turned and walked out of the door.

"Just a minute!" Skunk said. "You got one chance. It's so far out in the clouds that it ain't hardly worth mentioning, but there is a chance."

"What is that?" Rogett asked coldly, looking at the waiting Indians.

"You can let me talk for you. Tell him that his son shot at you first—though there ain't an Indian in this part of the world that knows what self defense means—and you can challenge his cowardliness. I'll tell them that his son shot at you from a hidin'-place. That he didn't show himself to you like a true brave. You can spit on the whole family—and say the whole family is a coward—

121

and maybe—maybe—they'll give you a chance to fight for your freedom."

Rogett swallowed. "Is that the only way?"

"Even that might not work."

Queen stepped up beside Rogett. "Sure, Skunk. See if you can get Meathead to go along with it. I'd like to see this lily skinned out of his hide while he's still standing."

Rogett turned and looked at Queen. He nodded, then suddenly shot out a clean right hand and caught Queen on the point of the jaw. The ramrod dropped to the floor and tried to rise. Rogett stepped in quickly and kicked him in the face. Again Queen tried to get up. Rogett, his face twisted, jumped high and came down on Queen's stomach. The man screamed and lay still.

Not a man moved in the room. Kantrell and Skunk looked at Rogett as if they had never seen him before.

Rogett turned to Skunk. "Make me a good deal, Skunk," he said and stepped out of the door.

The men poured out of the house and lined up along the front. Skunk and Rogett advanced toward the waiting Indians.

"Don't show 'em anything but that you're hell and the devil all in one suit, Mist' Rogett. If they get the idea that you're just doing this to save your life, they won't go for it. You've got to make 'em think that to lick you would be some hell of a big thing they could brag about. It wouldn't hurt for you to walk around them and look them over while I'm doing the talking. You might even spit in one of their faces. And strut a little. Put your hands on your hips and things like that. And I don't mind telling you that I'm skeered clean to hell and gone. Hold tight to your leather . . . here we go."

Chapter Eighteen

"MIST' ROGETT," Skunk said.

Rogett did not hear. He was moving around the three braves standing in back of the old chief, examining them as if they were freaks in a sideshow.

"Mist' Rogett!" Skunk said.

"What is it?"

"You did such a good job of making them mad with your prancing ways, they all want to fight you. They have to make up their minds which one it's going to be. The old chief is arguing with them now. The three others is some kind of relations or something. We're just going to have to stand here and wait."

"How do Indians fight?" Rogett asked.

"Catch as catch can. And then no holts barred. Knees, biting, scratching, gouging, hair pulling—anything. My, they sure are mad. They're about to get into a fight theyselves, just to see which one will take you on."

"I've never fought in my life, Skunk," Rogett said.

"Hell of a time to start learning," Skunk said, with a backward glance at Rogett. "It'll probably be with knives."

"I don't have a knife."

"Take mine," Skunk said. "Hold the blade up, and fight with it like it was a sword."

"I've done a bit of that," Rogett said. "Fencing."

"Fencing?"

"With the rapier."

Skunk frowned, all the while keeping his eye on the

jabbering Indians. "Is that that long thin sword, like a needle?"

"Yes."

"Then that's just dandy! There's hope yet."

"Can I expect tricks?"

"Everything in the book, from sand in the eyes, to screams and hollers to throw you off guard."

The Indians had become silent.

"They made up their minds. I hope it ain't that big bastid!" Skunk said.

Rogett waited. He held the knife in his hand and tried to go back, briefly, to his lessons with the rapier. It was hard. He could not remember a thing. There was so much to remember.

The largest of the Indians faced him. He had stripped to the waist and pulled his knife. Skunk moved out of the way. On the other side, seventy or eighty braves, still mounted on their ponies, moved in closer. Kantrell, Tasi and the men from the ranch house edged out to watch.

"You're at it, Mist' Rogett. Watch him. He's got a sly look about him. And whatever you do, don't let go that knife. They were born with a knife in their hands. An unarmed man might as well cut his own throat."

The brave began to advance toward Rogett. Wordlessly, silently, moving on the balls of his feet, dancing lightly. He hunched over, keeping his stomach away from a thrust, extending his knife, holding out his open palm for defense.

Rogett slipped into his own stance. It was the only one he knew. He would fight the man on his own terms, he said to himself, and it would be the best he could do.

Then slowly, as he moved, the memory of the lessons of years ago came back to him. The one thing he remembered was that with a rapier, a thrust could be made while parrying your opponent's blade.

He stood sideways, his left arm behind his back for balance, his right arm and the ten-inch blade extended.

The Indian lunged. Rogett slashed with his blade, got inside the lunge and slashed the forearm of the Indian. It was a bad cut. The blood began to flow down over the knife.

It was silent. Neither side said anything. There were no words of encouragement, no sighs or groans. It was a dusty silent fight to the death underneath the blazing noon sun.

The Indian became more wary. Rogett's right hand was like a snake—never still, ever moving in a slow circle up and around, watching his man and the blade that was now covered with the Indian's blood.

The Indian lunged in again. It was faster than anything Rogett had ever seen, and it was not with the knife hand but the free hand.

In a flash, Rogett, sidestepping, came forward with his left foot and kicked the free hand that had sought his right wrist. Dust flew in the Indian's face, blinding him momentarily, and Rogett was free, dancing away.

He was never the aggressor. He had learned a defensive weapon that could only attack when being attacked. It was the way he was taught. He had never gotten to the stage where his lessons would have taught him how to mount an attack.

But he was nothing now, if he could not attack. He could slash and keep the Indian off, but eventually, Rogett's mind told him, the Indian would get him.

He began to move in, catching the brave by surprise. The Indian made a wide pass with his blade. Rogett simply drew his forearm up and back and saw the blade pass harmlessly on around.

Like a triphammer his right forearm came down and caught the arm of the Indian again, cutting it to the bone. The brave staggered. The bone was laid open.

He backed up and switched the blade to his left hand. This caused a reaction among the Indians and they murmured.

There was a little talk on Rogett's side now. They were beginning to take hope. The Indian's arm was slashed to ribbons and Rogett had not gotten a scratch.

A natural fighter, gifted with coordination and skill

125

from years of training, the Indian was quick to adapt himself to the awkwardness of fighting with his left hand.

Rogett continued to fight his defensive battle, waiting for a chance to move in.

The Indian made another lunge, stumbled and nearly fell. Rogett again stepped in and kicked, catching the Indian on the side of the face and sending him sprawling. But before he could get in on top of him and finish him off, the brave was up and facing him again.

Slowly, steadily, Rogett began to mount his attack on the left-handed Indian. He would lunge, slashing at the knife hand, using his dragging foot for balance, pressing in. The Indian wanted to get in close for an infighting stroke at the gut, but Rogett kept moving away, keeping that long arm and the ten-inch blade between himself and the Indian.

Blood was streaming steadily from the brave's useless right arm now. The reflexes were astonishingly good, but still, Rogett saw, they were not quite as good as before. The man had lost too much blood.

He waited, carrying his pressing attack, with that slashing right arm and the blade in and out, anticipating every move of the Indian. He saw what he could do now, to win the battle.

"What is the worst name I can call him?" Rogett asked Skunk without looking at the old man.

"Mother boy," Skunk said, and then repeated it in Apache.

"Mother boy!" Rogett said, trying to ape the words that Skunk had used. His Apache was terrible, but it was enough to send the Indian in front of him into a frenzy.

"Careful," Skunk said. It was the only time anyone had spoken to him directly.

Rogett kept repeating over and over the needling words.

Again and again the Indian started to lunge after Rogett after hearing the phrase, and each time he drew up just short of the blade in Rogett's fist.

Then he moved forward again. It was exactly what

Rogett had been waiting for. He stepped in, arm extended fully, the blade an extension of his hand, wrist, forearm, and shoulder.

It was a clean thrust and the blade went into the Indian's stomach just below the rib cage and protruded from the other side.

Rogett held on to the blade and let the Indian fall off the edge, cutting upward as the man slumped over.

He looked up at the others. "What do I do now, Skunk?" he asked, holding the bloody knife in his hand.

"See that little bag around his neck?"

"Yes."

"Cut it off and empty it on the ground and then step on it. Then walk away, but not before you wipe the blade on the buck's breech clout."

Rogett did as he was told.

"Now pay respects to a brave Indian, but don't do it without a swagger and a strut like you had before. Give the knife to the old chief and then come back and pick up the dead Indian's knife. The idea is that you faced a brave man and hope that his blade will be a brave blade for you, but at the same time you're giving them the winner. Ain't nothing they like better than a winner."

Following Skunk's instructions, Rogett gave his blade to the chief. He then picked up the blade from the hand of the dead Indian and walked back toward the ranch house.

The Indians turned their ponies away from the cleared area and rode away.

They were hardly out of sight when the men in the yard, both those Rogett had hired and Kantrell's men, broke out into lusty cheers.

Chapter Nineteen

"I'VE FOUND THE TREASURE of Aahasi, Kantrell," Rogett said. "I know exactly where it is and how to get at it and I don't think that after what happened today Meathead will try to prevent me from setting up mining operations. So I am just as pleased that you have taken my check and that the contract is binding."

They sat in the dining room, the same dining room he had sat in the first night at the ranch.

Kantrell nodded. He had said nothing since Rogett had fought and killed the Indian brave. His whole manner was that of a man beaten at his own game.

"The contract is legal, you've accepted my money, and there isn't anything you can do about it. And if you attempt to prevent me in any way, Kantrell, I'll kill you. You made one mistake about me. You forget that I was a civilized man. It is not as difficult for a civilized man to revert to original orders as it is for a primate to think like a civilized man."

Skunk, who was sitting across the table, roared with laughter.

"All right," Kantrell said through his teeth. "You've won and I've lost. Now get the hell out of my house."

"Not quite yet, Kantrell," Rogett said, with iron in his voice. And now that Skunk thought about it, there wasn't a lot of difference between the man sitting at the table now and the man that had ridden off into the darkness and coolly shot two Apache Indians with a pop gun. There was very little difference between the two men.

"There is still something to be discussed," Rogett added.

"What?"

"Tasi," Rogett said easily. "Shall we talk about Tasi?"

Kantrell looked at Rogett and there was fire in his eyes. "Don't push me too far, Rogett."

"I'll push you just as goddamn far as I want to, Kantrell. Do you know why? Because you're greedy. You've probably been searching all your life for the treasure of Aahasi and never found it. And you know it must be a fantastic fortune. Well, it is. And your percentage will come to much more than you now own."

Kantrell was watching him closely. "What about Tasi?"

"We're going to be married."

"Married!" Kantrell half rose from the table and stared at Rogett, his mouth open. He turned to Tasi. "Is this true, Tasi?"

Tasi's voice was firm. "Yes. And I hope you aren't foolish enough to try and prevent it."

"He can't prevent it," Rogett said. "But I don't think he will even try."

They were silent. Skunk was busy with coffee and a huge chunk of steak. Outside, the men Rogett had brought from town and Kantrell's own men were finishing up their meal. They were laughing and talking. Their voices drifted into the big house.

"There are a few things that have to be cleared up, Kantrell," Rogett said. "For one thing, I want to know about Jezebel."

Skunk looked up sharply. "I wouldn't want to get into anything like that, Mist' Rogett."

Rogett paid no attention to the remark, but looked at Kantrell. "You might as well know," the rancher said slowly, "since you're going to marry Tasi—"

He looked at the dark-haired girl. "Whether you want to believe it or not, Tasi, you're my daughter. Certainly there is a lot of hokum surrounding our lives, and I'm guilty in a way. It was a way I had of keeping her alive for me. I wonder if you can understand that? I know it's been hard on you—"

129

Kantrell rose and walked to the window. He looked out over the flats and into the distance to the hills. "She was a wild woman, Mister Rogett. She told me she was going to leave me. Told me to my face. Long before the Indian came."

Rogett glanced over at Tasi. There was no expression on her face. It was like a person waiting for the crack of doom. "What did she tell you?" Tasi demanded.

"She said she'd leave me at the drop of a hat if a better man came along. That was all there was to life, Jezebel said. She said it many times. That was the fascination, I guess. She was the most honest creature I've ever met in my life. She said what she thought, and her thoughts were as simple and as true as the sun that rises and the rain that comes in the spring—"

He paused a long time. "All there was to life," he said. "She said it many times. All there was—for a man to have a woman and a place to sleep and something to eat and clothes to wear in the cold. Like animals. She didn't want big houses and diamonds and clothes—she wasn't like any other woman in the world."

Rogett, Tasi and Skunk were listening intently.

"You had to wake up, Jezebel would say, and root out your man for the day. And he had to be someone you looked up to. When the Indian, Aahasi, came in that day, saying those crazy things, I knew it was the way she wanted it."

"What did you do after she left?" Rogett asked softly.

Kantrell's voice became bitter. "I went looking for them. I searched those hills for months."

"Did you find them?" Rogett asked.

"Yes—you might say. They found me. I was starving to death, ran out of water, my horse went lame. I had been wandering around in the hills for maybe a week. Aahasi found me—and took care of me. I passed out, then when I woke up, Jezebel was there. She was pregnant. She told me it was my child."

Tasi listened, clenching and unclenching her hands on the table.

"She promised me that if I wanted to settle here in the valley, which was full of Apaches then—I would be safe. Aahasi would see to it that no one bothered me."

Kantrell stopped. "That's about all there is to it."

"Tasi," Rogett said gently, "any mystery is as profound as any other—until the simple answer is known."

Kantrell nodded. Tasi said nothing. Her face was stark white.

Slowly, piece by piece, Rogett told Kantrell of what had happened to Tasi and himself while they were in the hills. He told of discovering the cave and the gold—and the two skeleton figures. And he mentioned the bullet holes in the back of each skull. He told Kantrell about the mysterious helper who had provided them with horses, food, water and a route out of the hills, after digging them out of the cave. Kantrell and Skunk listened intently. Neither of them spoke until Rogett had finished.

Kantrell's voice was solemn. "I swear—on your heart, Tasi—that I don't know who the people were—the ones in the cave."

"Dug you out, huh?" Skunk said. "Well, I'll be damned! That's the damnedest story I have ever heard in my whole and entire life!"

"It's true. Every word of it," Rogett said slowly, watching Kantrell. "We would have been dead this minute if someone hadn't dug a tunnel through the rockslide to get us out. And I am not accusing you, Kantrell, of knowing the two people we found dead—inside. I don't even suggest who they might be."

Kantrell was silent a moment. "Who dug you out?"

"I don't know. I thought you might be able to tell me."

"Coulda been Meathead's bucks, determined to get you out of there and—" Skunk speculated slowly, pulling at his upper lip—"something scared them off. They would be the only ones that would have horses and water—and after killing old Meathead's son, you weren't around at the time, but he was sure mad as hell, and he coulda sent in his bucks to dig you out and something

pulled them off before they got to you—inside the cave."
He looked over at Kantrell for help with his proposal.
Kantrell said nothing. "And besides that, you saw how
determined the old bastard was to have at you—or any
live 'un—" Skunk's voice trailed off to a soft whisper. No
one said anything. "Well, it was a suggestion anyways,"
the old man said defensively.

Rogett pursed his lips. "Whoever it was has had some
mining experience at one time or another—very good
experience—because it took a very good man, knowing
what he was doing, to dig that tunnel without having it
cave in on him."

No one said anything.

"And there is the mystery of the two skeletons in the
cave—who may or may not be Aahasi and Jezebel." Rogett pressed the point just a little and watched them all.
All of them reacted as if pricked with a needle. "Any
ideas?"

"What makes you think it might be them?" Kantrell
insisted.

"Who else could it have been? With the treasure in
the back of the cave? Wouldn't you believe that if it was
anyone else, anyone at all, even Indians, they would
know the value of the treasure?"

Kantrell nodded. It was the slow, patient nod of a man
that has come painfully, finally to a decision. "Of course,"
he said.

"Of course what?" Rogett asked.

"Murdered. That's why I didn't see them again. After
they sent Tasi down to me in the valley." Kantrell could
hardly speak. The emotion was locked in his throat. "I
wanted to be friends with them. I often went back into
the hills looking for them. I had Tasi—she was enough—
but—I never saw them again. Then years passed—
more—" Kantrell spoke as if to himself, his eyes fixed,
studying a distant scene that only he could see. "And all
the time they were dead." He looked up at Rogett, the
expression that of a child. "But who—?"

There was a moment of hesitation, then Rogett looked

across the table. "Skunk," he said quietly.

"Skunk!" Kantrell said. "What do you mean? What has he got to do with it?"

"I'm not exactly sure, Kantrell. How about it, Skunk?"

Skunk was laughing. "Mist' Rogett, I still say you remind me of that feller down to Lane County. Yummy-mouthed feller, he was sure a talker. Said that he could sweet-talk any woman in the world to dropping her drawers if she would only give him her ear for a few minutes. You must be out of your goddamn mind!"

"That sweet-talking, yummy-mouthed feller from Lane County is you, isn't it, Skunk? And you sweet-talked Jezebel, didn't you, Skunk?"

"Mist' Rogett—"

"That's impossible!" Kantrell said. "Skunk only came to work for me a few years ago!"

"The night that I killed Meathead's son, when I tried to get into town, Kantrell, we were holed up here in the house when you returned, weren't we?"

"Yes, but—"

Rogett was watching Skunk. The man was staring back at him.

"Skunk told me everything that happened that day in the saloon when Aahasi walked in. He told it to me, like —like he was there! He told me, not as a man will who's repeating a story, Kantrell, but as a man will that was there and saw it and has found someone that has never heard the story before and is telling them everything. A man that likes to talk. A yummy-mouth, as he puts it."

Skunk was silent. Kantrell was looking at the old man as if he were searching for some thread that could lead him to believing that what Rogett was saying was true. He shook his head.

"Skunk is the only one that claimed to be a friend to everyone, Kantrell. To Tasi, me, Bet, and even you. He changed sides so often, it's a wonder he didn't get confused. No one would suspect old Skunk—not in a million years. A stable man—an old waddy that has finally come to hanging around a ranch and is satisfied to take what

133

he can get to keep himself in food and clothes and a place to sleep. Who would suspect old Skunk? I'll bet you don't even know his real name, do you Kantrell? Do you?"

Kantrell stammered. "Why—I don't know—Betajack keeps the names of the hands for the payroll—"

Betajack Queen appeared in the doorway, half bent over, holding his stomach. It was the sudden appearance of the ramrod that diverted Rogett's attention from Skunk for the moment needed by the old man to jump up and pull out a .45.

"Mist' Rogett," Skunk said, leveling the .45. "You still remind me of that feller from Lane County, Texas. He couldn't keep his mouth shut either."

Chapter Twenty

"PUT DOWN THAT GUN, you old bastard!" Bet said in his voice of authority.

"Just still yourself, Bet. I'd hate like hell to blow a hole in you, but I sure as hell will."

Kantrell was watching the old man now. Skunk turned his gaze around to face him. "You don't remember me, do you, Kid?"

Kantrell gasped at the use of the old nickname. "Should I know you?"

"Angus Fritchie," Skunk said. "I was your bartender—I worked for you and Jezebel."

Kantrell was still trying to place the name and the face.

"But then I sent that Indian in after Jezebel and quit."

"You did what!" Kantrell demanded.

Skunk laughed. He looked around the table. "Surprised, ain't you, Kid? You too, I guess, Bet, Tasi—and Mist' Rogett. Though Mist' Rogett only lately got all mixed up in this—question of Jezebel."

"Say that again," Kantrell demanded, rising up out of his chair.

"Sit tight, Kid. I'll blow hell outa you the same way you used to take on the tough cow waddies that drifted in the saloon and got fresh with Jezebel."

"You said you sent the Indian in—what do you mean by that?" Kantrell demanded.

"I mean, Kid, that me and Jezebel wanted to get out. I knew that to leave you behind would only mean that we'd have a horny old ding bat on our trail and that we'd get no peace as long as you were alive. Jezebel wouldn't let me blow you in half with a shotgun like I wanted to. So I went up into the hills—which by the way is how I came to this country in the first place—I used to look for gold when I was a young man—and knew there was gold in the hills if I just kept looking for it long enough. But I got tired of living alone and had to come down into Jicarilla for a little spell—and while I was in the hills I made fine friends with the Indians. Why, fer God's sake, I knowed old Meathead all my life and him knowing me about the same time. Aahasi and me used to hunt together before I ever saw you. But the first time I went down into town, I saw Jezebel—and well, you might say that Jezebel saw me. Hell, kid, we were playing you for the back door for a long time before I decided to get Aahasi to go to town and do something about it. Ain't you ever wondered, Kid, why she went along with Aahasi so nice and easy?"

Skunk stopped his long ramble, and Rogett knew by the look on both their faces that an old feud was out in the open at last.

"I remember you now, Skunk. You *are* Angus Fritchie. And you always were a no-good, sneaky sonofabitch!"

"Don't get mad, Kid. Life's over. Fer both of us. You been taken! You and that fast gun of yours. And when your finally came into the hills looking for Jezebel and Aahasi, it was easy as pie to steal your water at night, a little bit at a time, until you were plumb out of your head, and then have Aahasi come in and make things nice and easy for you."

"You're a goddamn liar!" Kantrell said.

"No I ain't, and deep down in your heart, you know I ain't lying. Why, Kid, Jessie—that's what I called her, I didn't like the name of Jezebel—Jessie and I used to sit up there in the hills and watch you down on the flats, straining and sweating, building up your empire and all for our daughter—"

"Your daughter!" Kantrell stared at Tasi.

"Yup. When Aahasi and Jezebel found you, we already had a problem about what to do with the child that was coming. Our child. And when you showed up, why it was easy to make you think that it was yours and Jessie's—Jezebel's—and have you take care of her and raise her proper and all and with education—which I thank you for. She's a fine girl. Though I understand she hates your guts. Can't say that I blame her though."

"You're a goddamn liar!" Kantrell screamed.

"No I ain't, Kid, and if you'd have ever stopped to count time instead of cattle, you'd have known that it was exactly thirteen months from the time that Jezebel left you with Aahasi and the time you came looking for her in the hills. Now how in hell can you figure her to be your younggun? Why, if I had a naked shave, you'd see she looks like me." Skunk looked at Tasi. "I'm sorry, child, that you had to learn it this way. But that's all there was to do when this yummy-mouthed feller you wanta marry started talking. If I had known it was going to end up like this, I never woulda got you two out of the cave."

"What about the two skeletons—the man and the woman, in the cave," Tasi demanded. "Who are they?"

"Two people Kid Kantrell shot in the back of the head when he was a gun in town years ago. Did he tell you he was a fast 'un? Well, he wasn't fast. I coulda beaten him to a stand-up showdown any time. His speed was shooting people in the back of the head, wasn't it, Kid. Look at him. He can't deny it even now."

Kantrell was staring at the old man as if he were a figment of the imagination rather than flesh and blood. "Oh, once in a while some slow old doddering cowboy would come through and be drunk enough to draw on Kantrell and he would gun him down, but generally, he wasn't anything but a no-good. Only reason I didn't kill him years ago was that Jezebel sorta felt sorry for him."

"You're a liar! This whole thing is a pack of lies!" Kantrell could hardly control himself. But he made no

137

move against the hard hand of Skunk and the .45 that was held in it. "She loved me—she loved me. She wouldn't run out on me for the likes of you!"

"You can rail against me all you want, Kid, like I said. Jessie, well, she got the fever some time back and died. I buried her up in the hills and decided I might as well come on down and square up with you. But when I got here, I just never got around to doing anything about it."

Skunk grinned at Rogett. "You might say I was sorry for him."

"Does that explain why you were able to talk Meathead into fighting one of their braves?" Rogett asked softly.

"Yup. I told that old bastard that if he didn't give you a chance, I'd hunt him down and shut both his eyes with a .45." Skunk laughed. "He knows me long enough to know that I would, too."

"Then you—you are my true father?" Tasi said.

"Every word I spoke here is the God's truth, child. Your mother was Jezebel Fritchie from New York City. She's got people back there, so have you. Her maiden name was Chance. Jezebel Chance—your real name is Tassandra Jezebel Chance Fritchie. And anytime you want to, I'll take you up into the hills and show you your mother's grave where I carved the headstone and it says: Here lies Jezebel Chance Fritchie, beloved wife of Angus Fritchie, lived as man and wife without being wed, but wed in the sight of God. Mother and father of Tassandra Jezebel Chance Fritchie, known as Tasi Kantrell."

Kantrell had listened to the story with the color slowly leaving his face. He wet his dry lips with his tongue.

"If you're Angus Fritchie, tell me this—" Kantrell asked. "Why did Aahasi say the things he did about the treasure and—"

Skunk chuckled. "Oh, that was just something we made up. Me and Jessie and Aahasi, sitting up there in the cave one night after we had discovered the gold lode, and a long time before we left Jicarilla. We used to meet up there in the hills in secret and after I found the gold, we had to make a decision, Kid. There we had all the money a man could want—go to New York, London, Paris—just live it up. Or, we could stay right up there in the hills and have just as good a life. All we needed was to be together. But we felt we had to give you a sporting chance. And it was Aahasi that figured out the saying, knowing that the idea of gold would get to you. I never saw anybody as greedy as you in my whole life, Kid. And that's the straight goods. You just never seemed satisfied with what you had, always had to have more and more and more—"

"I suppose you can prove everything you've said, Skunk," Rogett said. "I have an interest in this too, you know. I want to make Tasi my wife."

"I can't give you letters and deeds, Mist' Rogett. But I can trot out every squaw in old Meathead's tribe. I can even get Aahasi to back up my story, but he's pretty old now. Don't get around much. As a member of the Apache council—tribe wise men—he stays pretty close to his lodge pole—crippled up in the legs a bit too, after a ruckus with a bear. But he's alive and kicking and will back me up—and then there's all the women in Meathead's lodge that used to come begging around Jessie— Jezebel—and the old woman that borned Tassandra here, she's still living. Matter of fact, she goes into Jicarilla all the time. You probably seen her a dozen times, Kid. At least a dozen. Might even have said how-de-do to her." Not once in the long talk, as the story unfolded, did the .45 waver or was Skunk off guard.

Skunk laughed soundlessly. "Well, any more questions? I tell you, Bet, you too Kid, it's been a hell of a lot of fun. Sorta took my mind off Jessie. No harm done. And I can leave now that I know that Tasi had the gumption to stick by a real man when one came along. And he's a real man, daughter, don't ever think otherwise just because he talks fancy."

"Leave? Where will you go?" Rogett asked.

"Back into the hills," Skunk said. "I might get around to see you if you start up the mine operations, but I'll go on back and tell Aahasi all about what has happened." Skunk laughed. "He'll get a big bang out of all this. Has a sense of humor like a white man, not like an Injun at all. Best friend I ever had."

Skunk slipped out of the window, ducked down below the ledge, and ran hard across the front porch and leaped onto a horse. He was halfway across the clearing before Kantrell could get to the window and shoot.

It would be useless to follow him and they all knew it.

"I wonder if he's telling the truth. You can't believe an old man like that, Tasi. You just can't. I'm your father!" Kantrell insisted.

"Can you prove that you are?" Tasi asked.

"But he doesn't have any proof either!" Kantrell yelled.

"Well, someone had to dig us out of that cave. Someone, as Sidney said, who knew mining. And you remembered him. You remembered him," Tasi said.

She turned to Sidney. "Let's get away from here. I never want to see this place again as long as I live."

"Stop them, Bet. Stop them!" Kantrell yelled.

Betajack Queen shook his head. "Not me, Mister Kantrell. Any old timer that has enough gumption as Skunk wouldn't let me or anyone else get away with doing anything to Miss Tasi. You oughta know that by now."

"Well, if you won't, I will!" Kantrell screamed. He pulled out the gun. There was an explosive roar and a moment later a second.

Rogett had pulled the trigger a moment after he had seen Kantrell's move. The man slumped to the floor holding his stomach.

Bet did not move.

They stood. Tasi, Rogett, Bet, with the windows full of men who had crowded in when Skunk had made his run for the hills. They stood and watched Kantrell try to pull the gun up and aim it at Rogett.

The gun came up . . . higher . . . higher. Then it stopped, wavered.

Kantrell fell over backwards, the gun falling to the floor.

Rogett leaned down and picked it up. "He said he had stolen it from a wrangler pushing cattle into the grass country of Montana." He examined the old gun.

"He stole everything he has. Millions," Tasi said. "Millions."

"Except the one thing he really wanted was stolen from him," Bet said.

Suddenly Tasi began to cry. "I can't help it. I can't help it—he—he was all the father I knew—"

"It all seems so simple now," Betajack Queen said, rubbing his stomach.

"What does?" Rogett asked.

Bet looked up. "Why, the question of Jezebel."

WESTERNS

☐	AMBUSH AT JUNCTION ROCK—MacLeod	P3471	1.25
☐	THE APACHE HUNTER—Shirreffs	P3479	1.25
☐	BARREN LAND SHOWDOWN—Short	13659-0	1.25
☐	BOWMAN'S KID—Shirreffs	13599-3	1.25
☐	CHARRO!—Whittington	13703-1	1.25
☐	CIMARRON JORDAN—Braun	P3201	1.25
☐	DAKOTA BOOMTOWN—Castle	P3521	1.25
☐	DAY OF THE BUZZARD—Olsen	P3530	1.25
☐	THE EASY GUN—Parsons	13712-0	1.25
☐	GRINGO—Foreman	13555-1	1.25
☐	THE GUNSHARP—Cox	13549-7	1.25
☐	HE RODE ALONE—Frazee	13581-0	1.25
☐	THE KID FROM RINCON—Moore	13612-4	1.25
☐	KING FISHER'S ROAD—Rifkin	13711-2	1.25
☐	A MAN NAMED YUMA—Olsen	13616-7	1.25
☐	THE MANHUNTER—Shirreffs	13728-7	1.25
☐	THE MARAUDERS—Shirreffs	13723-6	1.50
☐	SMOKY VALLEY—Hamilton	13677-9	1.50
☐	TO HELL AND TEXAS—Lutz	13597-7	1.25
☐	TOP MAN WITH A GUN—Patten	13705-8	1.25
☐	WHITE APACHE—Forrest	13754-6	1.25

Buy them at your local bookstores or use this handy coupon for ordering:

Louis L'Amour

THE NUMBER ONE SELLING WESTERN AUTHOR OF ALL TIME. Mr. L'Amour's books have been made into over 25 films including the giant bestseller HONDO. Here is your chance to order any or all direct by mail.

☐ CROSSFIRE TRAIL	13836-4	1.50
☐ HELLER WITH A GUN	13831-3	1.25
☐ HONDO	13830-5	1.50
☐ KILKENNY	13821-6	1.50
☐ LAST STAND AT PAPAGO WELLS	13880-1	1.50
☐ SHOWDOWN AT YELLOW BUTTE	13893-3	1.50
☐ THE TALL STRANGER	13861-5	1.50
☐ TO TAME A LAND	13832-1	1.50
☐ UTAH BLAINE	P3382	1.25

Buy them at your local bookstores or use this handy coupon for ordering:

BESTSELLERS